# Isabel's
# War

# Isabel's War

## Lila Perl

**LIZZIE
SKURNICK
BOOKS**

Brooklyn, New York

Printed in the United States
10 9 8 7 6 5 4 3 2 1

Please direct inquiries to:
Lizzie Skurnick Books
an imprint of Ig Publishing
392 Clinton Avenue #1S
Brooklyn, NY 11238
www.igpub.com

ISBN: 978-1-939601-36-0 (hardcover)
ISBN: 978-1-939601-27-8 (paperback)

# One

Here we are again at Shady Pines, which is really just a fancy name for this smallish summer hotel that everybody calls Moskin's.

We crunch into the gravel parking lot, my father at the wheel of the 1939 Packard and my mother beside him. She's checking her hair and makeup in the windshield mirror because her female cronies are sure to be scattered around on the lawn. Or they might be seated at card tables on the broad wraparound porch of Moskin's main house.

Am I still talking to either one of my parents? It's not clear. All I know is that I've been sitting here in the back seat in stubborn silence ever since we left the Bronx three hours ago.

My mother breaks the stillness between us. "Here comes Ruthie. Act like a lady instead of a spoiled child. How composed and mature Ruthie looks. There's a daughter that Minnie Moskin can be proud of."

Ruthie is a lot older-looking than last summer. She's still pale and moonfaced, with a button nose and gray eyes. Her short-cut taffy-brown hair drapes her cheeks. But Ruthie has a "settled" air about her. I think she'll probably look the same as this when she's thirty-eight, forty-nine, even in her sixties. Right now, of course, Ruthie and I are the same age, twelve.

"Isabel," Ruthie says softly, putting her head through the open window of the back seat. She's already said hello to my parents, greeting them politely as "Mr. Brandt" and "Mrs. Brandt." The Moskin family has been getting Ruthie ready to play the part of the perfect hotel hostess since she was eight. In fact, this year Ruthie is officially known as "the governess." She will be in charge of the younger children of the hotel guests, leading them in games and sports and even overseeing them at mealtimes in the children's dining room.

As soon as my father and one of the busboys from the grownups' dining room have emptied the car trunk of our luggage, Ruthie and I stroll off toward the room I'm going to occupy this year. We walk with our arms around each other's waists, heads together.

"Don't be mad at me," I beg, "about not wanting to come to Moskin's this year. It has nothing to do with you and me. It's really about my being too old for this place. There's not much for me to do here, with you working full time. But they refused to send me to camp. Every time I ask for anything my father gives me the same excuse. 'This is 1942. There's a war on!'"

"Well," Ruthie says philosophically, "there is. Everything's changed since Pearl Harbor. We don't even have a band this summer. A couple of the fellows from last year had such low draft numbers that they're already in uniform. And the others have gotten much better jobs, at least until they get drafted."

"I know, I know. You wrote me."

I think longingly of the four young "college men" who were so tantalizing to me last summer when I was only eleven. Miltie on the piano, Pinkie on the drums, Lou on the trumpet, and Bob on the saxophone—tall, dark, handsome Bob—who would have been my choice if I hadn't been nearly ten years too young for him.

"Soon all the boys will be in the army serving overseas," I lament. "Then what?"

"Then we'll just have to wait for them to come back," Ruthie says resignedly.

"They won't all come back," I reply darkly.

We've reached the steps of the long, narrow wooden porch of the "Annex," a row of eight guest rooms, one of which will be mine and one my parents'. Ruthie looks off into the distance. "I have to get back to work. I'm taking the littlest kids on a nature walk at two o'clock. Want to come along?"

"Um, no thanks. Tonight, though, what's on for tonight?"

"Dancing in the social hall," Ruthie says. "To the jukebox. We could practice the Lindy."

I nod, a little. Ruthie and I aren't much good at the Lindy. We tried it last year and didn't get very far. Besides, it won't be much fun trying to jitterbug to the music from a machine. More and more, I'm at war with this war.

There's a knock at my door, which is instantly shoved open by my mother. She's already changed into shorts and a knit polo shirt. This is her customary daytime outfit when we're in the country. Also, she's wearing ankle socks with white leather oxfords that have Cuban heels.

"You haven't changed yet, Isabel? Are you planning on returning to the city or what?"

"I wish I could, and you know it."

My mother sits down on one of the twin beds, which is covered with a worn-looking white candlewick bedspread.

"Isabel, I don't want any trouble these next few weeks. Your father has just about had it and he's ready to explode. Here you are at Moskin's, away from the baking sidewalks and the stuffy apartment. You have Ruthie, one of your oldest friends. You've known her what—four, five years. Get into your bathing suit. Go down to the lake. I'll be on the porch of the main house if you want me."

She's gone.

I stare critically into the mirror above the scarred wooden bureau. The furnishings at Shady Pines aren't exactly new or fancy. After all, this isn't the Plaza Hotel on Manhattan's Fifth Avenue. And now, with the war on, goods for the home front are already beginning to get scarce. It's hard to get everyday things like soap and matches, much less new furnishings, which the Moskins wouldn't spring for in any case.

In fact, they've already announced in their 1942 brochure that, as ration coupons will be required for sugar, coffee, and butter, they will no longer be able to serve unlimited quantities of these foods in the dining room. Everything, everything, is for the troops and is going for the war effort.

My reflection is still staring back at me. Why, oh why, I ask myself, did I have to be born with my father's nose? This is something that began to be noticeable during this past year. Especially since I was visited for the first time by the remarkable events outlined in that informative little booklet entitled "Marjorie May's Twelfth Birthday"—otherwise known as "getting your period."

Is it possible that "becoming a woman" means that you can begin to grow a nose like a man? Why didn't Arnold, my seventeen-year-old brother, inherit my father's nose? But no, blond, blue-eyed, and baby-faced Arnold (who is back home in the city working at a summer job) is the very picture of a romantic pretty-boy. While I...oh, what's the use?

All I've been asking for these past few months is a bobbing—just the tip of my nose pushed up and back, something I can do with my index finger, hardly what you would call a nose job.

But my parents have refused to listen to me, even forbidden me to bring up the subject. "There's a war on," says my father.

"What's that got to do with it?" I ask, falling right into the pit.

"Good heavens, Isabel," he thunders, "don't you think doctors have more to do than making your nose one-thirty-second of an inch shorter? Aren't you hearing on the radio what's been going on in the steaming jungles of the Philippines, Bataan, New Guinea? How can you be so thoughtless and selfish?"

Steaming jungles, hmm. It's plenty hot in this little wooden box of a room that's supposed to save me from the baking sidewalks of *Le Grand Concours.* That's French, in case you didn't know it, for this big busy street in the Bronx, lined with apartment buildings, that's known as The Grand Concourse. As Miss Le Vigne, my French teacher, would say, *"Mon dieu, ouvrons les fenêtres. Comme il fait chaud!"*

But there are no windows to open. The only window is at the back of my little room, and it's already open and looks out onto a barricade of dark pine forest heavy with trapped air. So I wriggle into my bathing suit, grab a coarse, pebbly towel, and wander down the path that leads across a dirt country road to the lake, better known as Moskin's Mud Hole.

Sure enough, there are a bunch of eight- and ten-year-olds, all boys, cavorting around the dinky wooden platform that is used as both a boat dock and a diving platform.

If there's anything I hate more than ten-year-old boys, it's twelve-year-old boys. Short, fat, and boisterous; skinny, freckled, and buck-toothed; tall, gangly, and pimpled—all twelve-year-old boys make me feel like I want to vomit.

The kids at the lake give me a passing but interested look as I glide by them. My breasts, along with my nose, have popped noticeably in these past couple of months, and I'm wearing a jersey two-piece bathing suit. Just one fresh remark, I think to myself, and I'll punch the little smartass right in the nose.

But Moskin's young guests soon return to scrambling up onto the dock, holding their noses, and plunging back into the water like a pack of trained seals, while I take off and slip into the lake at a more distant point, swimming slowly to the far shore. There are footpaths there that trail off into the woods and lead to clusters of rented summer bungalows. Moskin's, after all, doesn't own the entire lake, and you can tell this from the fact that here, where I'm now sitting on my towel and drying off, there's an old rubber swimming tube and a rowboat that's been pulled up onto the muddy shore.

It's probably not a good idea to go exploring along one of the footpaths today because I'm barefoot and already my feet have been cut by sharp stones from when I crossed the dirt auto road at Moskin's to get to the lake. Still, I'm sort of entranced by the path just to my left through the deep piney woods. It has to lead somewhere.

So maybe I'll wander just a little way in through the dimness, stepping softly on the pine needles that cover the dusty soil. It is dark in here, though. Not spooky, but not exactly friendly either.

What if there are snakes? That curved branch over there, for example. It could be a snake. Simply because it's lying so still doesn't mean it isn't a living slithery thing, just waiting to strike. I draw closer and peer down at it. How close do I dare get, and why am I being so dangerously nosy anyway?

Suddenly there's this strange rustling noise coming from somewhere nearby. It could have been a bird flying out of a tree. But when I look down I could swear that the "branch" on the ground has moved. Now, I really do have to satisfy my curiosity. Was that the warning rattler on a rattlesnake's tail that I heard rustling? Could there actually be rattlesnakes in the nearby woods threatening Moskin's juicy summer guests?

Softly, softly, I approach the snake/tree-branch. Not a sound, nothing stirs. And, then, in a flash, something springs up at me. It has no mouth, no flicking tongue, no venom-filled fangs, but surely it's alive.

I jump back as far as I can, stumble on some tree roots, and go sprawling on my backside. My head bangs hard as I hit the ground, and for an instant, everything goes black.

Then, slowly, the pain of a bruised elbow, a badly bumped shoulder, and a bonked head bring me to. I open my eyes to a startling whiteness and think instantly of the uniformed nurse who was standing over me when I had my tonsils out. But, no, I'm still in the woods. Only now I'm no longer alone.

"Gosh," says a soft male voice, "what happened to you, girl? Looks kinda like you dropped right outta the trees. Help you up?"

I am so embarrassed. I'm not really a klutz—one of those kids who's clumsy at everything and always falling down. And this, this person who's peering at me from above is the cutest sailor in the U.S. Navy that you ever saw. He's wearing his summer whites, middy and bell-bottom trousers, no cap, and has earnest brown eyes and dark hair. He reminds me a little bit of Bob, last summer's saxophone player in Moskin's band. And, of course, he's eighteen or so, and—just like Bob—probably too old for me.

He pulls me up with one hand and I brush myself off and say, "*Merci beaucoup*," trying to sound casual and not the least bit put out by my recent tumble.

"Are you French?" he asks, raising one eyebrow.

"Not really," I confess. "My name's Isabel."

We chat awhile as we walk back toward the lake. His name is Roy and he's a recent enlistee in the Navy. Right now he's visiting his family at one of the bungalow colonies and he's awfully bored—and wondering what there is to do around here…

A few minutes later I'm hurrying back to Moskin's. I can't wait to tell Ruthie that I met a sailor in the woods and that he's coming to Moskin's casino tonight to dance to the jukebox. (Oh, about that "snake"—it was just a weirdly curved greenish-black tree branch, after all.)

# Two

Still in my slightly damp bathing suit, I'm looking all over Moskin's for Ruthie. This sailor boy, Roy, really looks groovy to me. I'll bet he can do the Lindy. And he doesn't seem to have that supercilious attitude toward twelve-year-old girls that my brother Arnold has. So maybe, war or no war, the summer at Shady Pines won't get off to such a dreary start after all.

The best place to find Ruthie when she isn't taking care of the guests' kids is in the hotel kitchen. When I was younger, I have to admit, it was my favorite hangout, mainly because of the crock, always filled with big thick cookies topped with cinnamon and sugar or with chocolate sprinkles that were there for the taking.

Sure enough, Mrs. Moskin, Ruthie's mother, who's in charge of the kitchen and does most of the hotel cooking, spots me with a nod of her chin toward the cookie jar. As usual, she's wrapped in a white apron that looks like flour sacking and wears a head cloth that completely covers her hair. Even her pale eyebrows and her broad-featured face appear to be dusted with flour.

Mrs. Moskin enfolds me in a warm, familiar hug. "About time you came in to say hello, Isabel. You were already at the lake? Take a cookie."

I guess I have been rude. It was always the custom in the past to greet Minnie Moskin the moment one arrived, and I'm sure my parents have already done so. It's just that I've been in such a bad mood over all the arguing with my parents and the war suddenly being an excuse for everything.

As to Ruthie, Mrs. Moskin tells me she's now having a story hour in the children's dining room. "Oh," I say, "then I won't bother her until after I change for supper. I have something interesting to tell her."

Mrs. Moskin smiles and nods approvingly, almost as if she knows about the sailor I met in the woods, who's coming to Moskin's this evening. But of course that's silly. How could she?

I trudge across the hotel grounds to the Annex. It's already getting toward late afternoon and there aren't many people around. Moskin's guests, the older ones anyway, often take afternoon naps before dinner and then make an early rush for the showers before getting dressed for the evening meal.

The door to my room is slightly ajar, which isn't surprising since nobody locks their doors at Moskin's and my mother may already have gone in and out several times. I just wish she'd shut the door, though, because Moskin's is the main haunt around here of bees, wasps, hornets, horse flies, and even bats.

I nudge the door wide open with my foot, already starting to undo my bathing suit top, when I'm struck by the presence of a tall young woman bending over a suitcase on the twin bed next to mine.

"Excuse me!" I say indignantly. "You're in the wrong room. This one is mine."

The figure across the tiny room turns. She's not quite old enough to be called a young woman. She's a girl, taller, skinnier, and older than I by maybe a couple of years. She has honey-brown hair that is long and wavy, a swan-like neck, and luminous gray-green eyes.

"Oh," she says, "you must be Isabel. I am Helga."

Her accent is a little strange, and automatically I say, "*Pardonnez-moi?*" French, as you can see, comes to me at the flick of an eye when I'm baffled.

"Helga," she repeats. "We will be roommates. You speak some French but I am sorry. I speak only German and the English I've learned living a few years now in the English countryside. I hope it will be good enough for us to have many conversations."

All this time I'm holding my detached bathing suit top up to my chest. Helga may be a girl close to my age, who even speaks my language, but she might as well be a menacing alien from Mars or even a Nazi storm trooper.

"Excuse me," I say, rapidly reattaching my bathing suit top. "I just remembered something."

Two seconds later I'm banging on the door of my parents' room, a short distance from mine in the annex. My mother, in her cotton pique summer negligee, opens it and peers out suspiciously.

"Oh, it's you. Why are you making such a racket? Your father is napping. How come you're still in your bathing suit?"

*She* is asking *me* questions. What nerve. I brush them all aside. "*Who* is Helga?" I demand. "What is she doing in my room, unpacking a suitcase on the other bed? You told me I was going to have my own room this summer." I know that I'm screeching out here on the annex porch. But I really don't care.

My mother reaches for my shoulder and hustles me across the threshold, while my father grunts irritably from one of the twin beds, where I've probably ruined his pre-dinner nap.

"It all happened while you were at the lake," my mother explains quietly but none too apologetically. She sits down on the other twin bed and motions for me to do the same. "You see, the Frankfurters arrived late this afternoon with this wonderful surprise, their niece." Harriette Frankfurter is my mother's best friend. "She was smuggled out of Germany in 1939 and has been living in England. They finally got her over here to live with them. She has no other family, poor thing."

"Okay," I say hesitantly. "But what has that got to do with me having to share a room, when I was promised I'd have one all to myself."

"Isabel, how can you be so selfish? For one thing, the Moskins are short of rooms right now. And Helga is fourteen. So she really shouldn't have to share with her aunt and uncle."

"Fourteen," I snap. "She's too old for me. I don't think we'd be such good roommates. And her English is kind of…well, stiff."

"Nonsense," my mother cuts in. "She's a lovely child. I had quite a conversation with her myself. You and Ruthie and Helga will make a wonderful threesome. And you'll have a companion when Ruthie is busy with her duties. Don't you have any feeling at all for somebody who's been through a terrible time in this war? Go back to your room and be as nice as you can to her. I'll see you at dinner."

I'm still grumbling to myself about *the war, the war,* and how it's causing so many problems and annoyances, when Helga and I cross over in the slanting sunlight to Moskin's main building where the dining room is located. Believe me, though, it's nothing fancy, just big and buzzing with noisy conversation, as the guests of

Shady Pines whet their appetites with glasses of tinkling water and vigorously tear apart Minnie Moskin's home-baked rolls.

Helga is wearing a flowered chiffon dress that is much too pretty and dressed up for the occasion. But I didn't say anything to her. Maybe it's all she has in the way of dress-up clothing. I have no idea what people have been wearing in wartime Germany and England, but I imagine it's something drab and practical.

We head for the big round table where my parents and Mr. and Mrs. Frankfurter, Helga's aunt and uncle, are already seated, watching our approach with appraising eyes. Everybody *oohs* and *aahs* at how lovely Helga looks. Before they can say a word about me, I spot Ruthie at the far end of the dining room where the Moskin family has its own table, and I dash off to tell her my news about Roy, the sailor I met in the woods.

Ruthie is having a quick bite because she has to watch the little ones while their parents are at dinner.

Ruthie's eyes widen. "Really? A sailor. How old do you think? Cute?"

"Very. You'll see. I'm sure he'll show up at the social hall later."

Ruthie nods in the direction of the table where Helga is sitting and chatting with my parents and her aunt and uncle. "What about *her*?"

"Oh, well, I don't think she's his type. She's sort of

foreign, you know. Anyhow, I'm still recovering from the shock of having her dumped on me like that. I was supposed to have my own room, you know."

Back at the table, my mother gives me a sour look. "What was so important that you had to tell Ruthie?" She turns to Helga. "You must excuse my daughter. Her manners…well, she tends to be a little impulsive."

Helga looks at me forgivingly. I doubt if she even knows the English word *impulsive*. Meantime, Harry the waiter is bearing down on us with a tray laden with plates of soup. Harry, with his polished black hair, his dark seamy face, his swirling dancer's movements, has been the headwaiter at Moskin's ever since I can remember.

"So Miss Isabel, who's your new friend, the beauty?" Harry asks me familiarly as he elegantly sets a brimming soup plate down in front of Helga.

"She's Helga. From Germany," I reply.

Harry is already halfway around the table, and my parents and the Frankfurters are filling in the details of Helga's presence at Moskin's. With his free hand, Harry lifts two fingers to his lips and tosses a kiss of approval in Helga's direction.

I turn to Helga. "Don't mind him," I tell her confidentially. "Harry is such an old flirt. He blows kisses to all the ladies around here. He does it for the tips, you know."

But Helga isn't really listening to me. Nor has she

touched her soup. She's looking up at one of the busboys who's been standing, mesmerized, just behind Harry's shoulder. I think his name is Ted. And Ted's gaze, in turn, is riveted on Helga.

*Aha*, I think to myself. So this is how it's going to be. Helga, the pale green-eyed beauty, the waif, the teenage princess from abroad, adored and admired by men from sixteen to sixty. And me, the twelve-year-old kid, with the semi-developed body, a mop of black hair, and a nose that's just crying out for a plastic surgeon who can be spared from the front lines.

The evening meal at Moskin's goes on much longer than usual tonight. People from other tables come over to talk to the Frankfurters and to question Helga with curious, pitying expressions on their faces. "Did you ever see Hitler, that bum?" one of the guests inquires.

Helga shakes her head, mouthing a silent no and explains that she lived in a medium-sized city in northern Germany before she was spirited away to England with other children of endangered or broken families. Nobody, of course, asks what happened to Helga's parents and the rest of her family in Germany. They may by now be in a prison camp or even dead. Probably no one really knows, not even the Frankfurters.

All this time, Helga has hardly eaten a thing. A few spoonfuls of soup, a chicken wing, some peas and carrots.

"You have no appetite?" another hovering Moskin guest wants to know. "No wonder you're thin as a rail."

To my surprise, Helga stares back at the woman almost angrily. "We don't eat like this in England, and not in Germany either before leaving. Here in America…."

Helga's Aunt Harriette breaks in apologetically. "What Helga's trying to say is that we haven't felt the brunt of the war here yet. Our food is much too rich for her after the wartime diet she's accustomed to."

Helga just lowers her eyes. "Thank you, Aunt Hattie," she says, after the nosy-body leaves the table, only to make way for others.

I suppose it is hard to be the center of attention, although of course *I* wouldn't know. The one thing that's on my mind at the moment is how late it's getting and what if Roy has already arrived at the Shady Pines social hall with nobody there to greet him.

"You'll all have to excuse me," I blurt out suddenly. "I just remembered something terribly important."

"Isabel," my mother says in a warning tone, "I hope you're not being rude."

"No, no," I assure her. "I'd be rude if I didn't take care of this…um, problem, right now."

I dash out into the lobby of the main building and look around quickly for a glimpse of Roy in his sailor garb. A few guests have already set up card games and others are sitting and talking in groups, the men smoking their after-dinner cigars. It's already dusk as I make my way across the bumpy lawns of Shady Pines, out past the Annex, and beyond it to the squat wooden building that was the scene of so much fun last summer. By this time in the evening, the band at Moskin's would have begun playing catchy tunes from the Hit Parade of 1941 and even earlier…peppy songs like "Boo Hoo" and "The Love Bug Will Bite You (If You Don't Watch Out)."

I race up the wooden steps of the casino, which is dimly lit and not very inviting from the outside. Would Roy even know that this was the fun palace with all the "action" that I described to him this afternoon? No-body is here, nobody, that is, except a handful of little kids, mainly the eight- and ten-year-olds from the lake. Some of them are fooling with the jukebox, trying to get it to play without putting money in. Others are jumping off the stage, scrambling back up, and jumping off again.

*"Quels stupides!"* I mutter under my breath. I grab one of the little boys. "Listen," I say, "did you see a sailor come in here, a young fellow in a white Navy uniform?"

"Nah," says the kid, with a snide grin. "Whaddya think, the fleet's in? Don'tcha know the whole U.S. Navy's in the Pacific fightin' the Japs?"

I turn away in disgust and go sit in the dark on the casino steps until Ruthie finally turns up a good half-hour later. She sits down beside me. "He didn't show, huh?"

"You're sure you didn't see him anywhere around the main building?"

"No, I looked everywhere on my way over here. He was probably too shy. Or he couldn't find his way in the dark."

"Or," I say, in quiet despair, "who's going to bother keeping a promise to a twelve-year-old girl with a chest that's too small and a nose that's too big?"

# Three

Early the next morning I'm awakened by the sound of stealthy but distinct movement coming from Helga's side of the room. I open one eye and glare at her. She's sitting on her bed fully dressed in very short khaki shorts, a heavy dark green sweater, and is pulling on a pair of leather lace-up hiking boots.

Her legs are entirely bare and, as she gets to her feet, I can't help noticing how long, slender and yet well-developed they are. "*Ach*. I'm sorry, Isabel, if I woke you."

*Ach*. This is the first expression in German that I've heard from Helga.

"Where are you going?" I ask suspiciously. "It's barely light out."

"To make a morning walk," she says, as if it were the most natural thing in the world to go tramping across the countryside two hours before breakfast. "You should come. It's very healthy. Shall I wait for you to dress?"

I turn over and fling the covers across my head. "No thanks," I wave at her with one hand. "I'll see you at breakfast."

But somehow Helga has wrecked my early morning sleep pattern. I toss around in bed for half an hour or so. Then I'm wide awake, so I get up and start wandering around our room. I know it's wrong of me, but I can't help poking through Helga's half of the closet and in the drawers of our shared bureau. From the way Helga looked last night in her flowered chiffon dress, I had no idea she was such an outdoorsy type.

Just as I suspected, she doesn't have much in the way of dress-up clothing. But she has lots of drab brown shirts, with military-looking epaulets on the shoulders, and short boxy skirts to match. She has several pairs of mud-colored socks and another pair of boots. It's almost as though Helga's been living in some kind of uniform.

And then there's the sturdy cardboard box in her top drawer that says *Schokoladen* on it. That's got to be German for chocolates. But it feels like it's packed with something much heavier. It would be easy to slip the cover off and take just one peek inside. But I know that would really be going too far. And yet…one peek… How bad would that be?

I open the door of my room and look out. The Annex porch is empty; the grounds of Shady Pines appear to be deserted. Hardly anyone is up yet. I tiptoe back to the mysterious chocolate box and gently lift up the deep-fitting cover.

There is an old photo right on top of a family, parents and very young children. Could one of them be Helga when she was little? Other pictures, too. And there are letters, still in their neatly slit-open envelopes, with canceled stamps and with addresses in foreign-looking penmanship. Carefully, carefully, I slide one of the letters out of its envelope. But I can't make out a word. It must be in German, and so must all the others.

I'm just sliding the letter back into its envelope when I hear a step on the annex porch followed by a soft knock at the door. I jam the cover back onto the chocolate box, slam the bureau drawer shut much too noisily, jump back into bed, and call out in the sleepiest voice I can muster, "Who's there?"

Whoever it is doesn't seem to have heard me, knocks again, and softly calls out in a woman's voice, "Helga, are you there?" This time, I get out of bed, go to the door, and open it to find Helga's aunt, Harriette Frankfurter, standing there with an apologetic smile on her face.

"Ooh, sorry if I woke you, Isabel. I need to speak to Helga."

Harriette Frankfurter is a bosomy redhead, a sort of little pouter pigeon of a woman who always rings her eyes with black eyeliner. At this hour of the morning she's already in full makeup, scarlet-lipped and dressed in a bright floral-patterned playsuit.

I open the door wide to show that I have nothing to

hide. "Oh, come in Mrs. Frankfurter. Except that…well, Helga isn't here."

Mrs. F. makes clucking noises of disapproval when I tell her that Helga has gone on a pre-breakfast hike. "Oh dear," she says. "It's all that marching around, first in Germany and then in England."

My mind flashes on the uniform-like wardrobe in Helga's half of the closet.

"You mean she was in some sort of army over there?" I inquire.

Mrs. F. nods. "In a sense. In Germany, before they found out she was half-Jewish, she was in one of those children's fitness clubs that later became part of the Hitler Youth. Then, of course, they threw her out. She was only nine. In England, she belonged to a youth group that was connected with the military. Long marches to build up the body. The child eats practically nothing, as you saw last night. I'm worried about her."

Helga's aunt sits down on the side of my bed. "So, tell me, are you two getting along all right? I hope you'll turn out to be good friends, even if there's a small age difference. Oh, and what I came to tell Helga this morning is that we'll be going into the village after breakfast to pick out some pretty summer clothes for her. Maybe you'd like to come along, Isabel? I'm sure you could help us find a few stylish outfits for Helga now that she's going to be living in America."

*Helga, Helga, it's all about Helga.* But, of course, I agree to go along on the shopping trip. What else is there for me to do? I know I've been mean and grumpy and unkind in my secret thoughts. Helga has had a hard time, surely. That picture of the mother and father and the three little girls. Where are they now? Was Helga one of them, and was she the only one who escaped the Nazis?

I'll try, honestly I'll try, to put myself in her shoes.

"So where's our pretty young lady this morning?" Harry the waiter wants to know as he flashes his way around the breakfast table with bowls of steaming farina and creamy-looking scrambled eggs. The table is loaded with fruit juices, grapefruit halves, toast, butter, jam, coffee, as well as cottage cheese, herring, and sour cream.

Helga has not returned from her morning walk yet. Twice I've been sent back to the annex to look for her and once Mrs. F. has gone herself.

"She doesn't know the countryside around here," Mrs. F. laments.

Mr. F., Helga's father's brother, pats his wife's hand. "Countryside is countryside. What's the difference whether it's over there or over here? The kid is an experienced hiker."

Everyone at the table keeps reassuring everyone else that Helga is fine and will be back at Moskin's any minute. But nobody is really convinced. "You should have gone with her this morning, Isabel," my mother remarks. "Her first time in a new place."

I throw an exasperated look in my mother's direction. I could like Helga a lot more if I wasn't constantly being reminded of something I should have done for her that I haven't. "No, no," Mr. and Mrs. F. break in, "it wasn't Isabel's responsibility."

Breakfast ends, and people stand around in a tight little knot trying to decide what to do and where to look for Helga. Some of the male guests volunteer to drive up and down the roads that snake in various directions leading away from Moskin's. Others offer to comb the countryside around the lake. Someone else suggests alerting the police in the nearby village of Harper's Falls.

Ruthie joins me, and we go off to the annex to act as sentinels in case Helga turns up and heads directly for her room. "Such a fuss," I remark disgustedly, as we actually go inside for another look around and then settle down on the steps of the porch. "I could be missing for three days and nobody would notice."

"You know that's not true," Ruthie says. "And Helga's been gone for close to three hours. Are you sure she was okay when she left?"

"Of course she was. You've got to get used to the fact that she's one of those outdoorsy types from Europe. When she says a 'morning walk' she probably means a ten-mile hike. I don't see why everyone is so worried. What could possibly happen to her?"

Ruthie glances at me sharply. "I never saw you in such a mean mood as this summer, Izzie. *Anything* could happen. *Everything* could happen. She could fall into a ditch and break a leg, she could start across a cow pasture and be charged by a bull, she could meet up with one of the inmates from the home for the feebleminded over in Boonetown and be…"

"Be what?"

"Well…attacked."

"You mean raped, don't you?"

"Not necessarily. Just, well you know, scared to death."

"I can't believe they'd let those people roam all over the place unless they were sure they were harmless."

"Well, that's what I mean. They could be harmless but Helga wouldn't know that. They drool a lot and they hold on really tight when they grab you…"

My hands go flying to my forehead. This *is* beginning to sound serious. I can already see Helga screaming with pain in a ditch beside the road where no one can see her or hear her, or clutching her stomach which has been gored bloody by a mad bull, or wrestling with some slimy-mouthed retard in a lonely clearing deep in the woods. How could I be so lacking in imagination, so completely blind to the terrible possibilities lurking in this new world to which Helga has come from so far away to be safe.

In the midst of all my mental turmoil, Ruthie is suddenly nudging me urgently. "Look, look. Is that him?"

I take my hands away from my forehead and follow her pointing finger. There, just at the corner of the annex, walking with a comfortable swagger in his dazzling sailors' whites in our direction, is none other than Roy. And beside him, trotting along rather slowly and with a bandaged left leg, is Helga.

Other people have also witnessed their approach. "Oh my goodness, it's our Helga," Harriette Frankfurter bursts out, tearing across the lawn from the main house. Ruthie and I are on our feet. People are coming together from all directions. Helga and Roy are soon encircled.

"You brought her back to us," Mrs. F. exclaims. "Oh, you dear boy. Where did you find her? She's limping and so pale. Helga, Helga, what happened to you?"

A chair is brought and Helga is lowered into it. Another chair appears and Roy gently lifts Helga's bandaged leg to rest on its seat.

"She wasn't hurt bad," Roy, clearly the hero, tells the crowd. "It was a farm dog. They can get pretty mean, though, you know. So when we heard all the barking and growling over at our summer place across the road, I started off for the farm. Sure enough, she was on the ground and he had her by the calf."

Mrs. F. is wringing her hands and Mr. F. is trying to steady her. "Helga is so frightened of dogs," her aunt says.

"The Nazis, you know. With their terrible killer guard dogs." Mrs. F. lowers her voice. "But we won't speak of that now."

*"Nein, nein,"* Helga whispers to the concerned faces bending over her. "Not such a big dog as in Germany."

Roy folds his arms and looks down on Helga with concern. "Big enough. And he really got his teeth into her. So I borrowed a car and took her into town. Got the doc to stitch her up and give her a tetanus shot. You never know with these farm dogs. He could have had rabies from a raccoon or even a bat. But the doc said no way."

By this time, Harriette F. has fainted and is lying on the grass being fanned by my mother and Mr. F. I turn to Ruthie. "Could she really get rabies?"

Ruthie shrugs. "The doctor would know if there was any chance of that." Her glance shifts to Roy. "Gosh, but he's awfully cute, Izzie. And to think you were the one to find him."

I roll my eyes. "A lot of good that does."

Roy has been invited to have lunch with us at the hotel. Helga, who has been resting most of the morning, is looking a little less ghostlike. But everyone is watching her for signs of rabies, just in case the tetanus shot didn't do the job.

Questions are directed at her by worried well-wishers

from all over the dining room. "How much does your leg hurt now?" "Is there any kind of burning sensation where you were bitten?" "Are you sure the wound isn't infected?" "Have you got a headache?" "Can you drink water?"

After Helga wanly assures everyone that she has no symptoms of rabies, interest focuses on Roy who, by now, admits to our meeting in the woods. He asks me how my "snake bite" is doing and did I remember to suck the venom out after I got back to Moskin's?

I don't think this is very funny. And it lands me in trouble with my parents. My mother immediately demands an "explanation" and promises that we'll "talk about this later." Which makes me feel like a baby in front of Roy and Helga, who are the golden couple at the table.

Both my father and Mr. F. want to know how come Roy enlisted in the Navy and whether he thinks it's better to choose your branch of service or wait to be drafted. I know my father is thinking about my brother Arnold, who's getting awfully close to being assigned a draft number. Roy, it turns out, is seventeen and just out of boot camp, which is why he's on furlough waiting for an assignment, maybe in the Pacific, maybe somewhere else. Helga gazes at him worshipfully as he relates his plans for the future. He is only a raw seaman at the moment, but he might as well be an admiral as far as she's concerned. And doesn't Roy know it? And isn't he just eating it up?

Lunch is finally over and Helga has been ordered by all the grownups to go back to her room and rest. Minnie Moskin herself comes out of the kitchen with a glass of half-milk and half-cream and a tray of her thick round cookies for Helga to take to her room. Mrs. F. carries the tray for her as she limps off toward the annex, while Roy stands looking after Helga wistfully.

I rush up to Roy, dragging Ruthie behind me, and I introduce them. "You should have come to the casino last night. We had such a great time," I tell him, poking Ruthie and crossing my fingers behind my back.

"Yeah," Roy sighs, his eyes still focused on Helga's slowly retreating figure. "But how was I supposed to know *she'd* be there? I figured it would just be a bunch of kids or a lot of older folks."

"Oh, thanks a lot," I reply. Even Ruthie looks hurt at Roy's remark. "So how long is this furlough of yours, anyway?" I ask the great lover.

"Just one more day."

*"Quel dommage!"* I know it's not nice of me but I just can't help it.

"Whatever *that's* supposed to mean," Roy mutters as he starts sauntering off...the last he'll probably see of Shady Pines.

# Four

"You shouldn't have cursed him in French like that," says Ruthie, as Roy disappears across the road. "He's fighting for our country. He could get killed in the Pacific. The Japanese are sinking our battleships right and left. Or don't you read the papers?"

"I don't. Not the way my father does. Who can remember the difference between New Guinea and Guadalcanal? And where in the world are the Solomon Islands? Anyhow, what I said to him wasn't a curse. *Dommage* is the word for pity, so all it meant was, *What a pity.*"

"It sounded," Ruthie insists, "like you called him a dummy. And very sarcastic, too."

Since Ruthie and I aren't exactly on the best of terms at the moment—and she has to take her little tykes off to the playground (two rope swings and a bumpy slide) after their naps—I go slouching off to the deserted social hall to practice piano. It's the best way I can think of to avoid waking Helga, who's supposed to be sleeping or at least resting.

I wish I didn't have such mixed feelings about Helga. It's stupid of me, of course, to be angry with her because of Roy. It isn't her fault that she ran into an unfriendly dog and that Roy came to her rescue. And it isn't her fault that there's a war on in which she's one of the victims, so that in this small world up at Moskin's, people are centering their feelings of sympathy on her.

I've been practicing my Czerny exercises for twenty minutes or so, when I hear a step behind me.

"Oh, I thought I heard tinkling noises in here."

I turn around. It's Mrs. F. She's changed out of her colorful playsuit and is wearing an orange blouse and a tan walking skirt. "I just looked in on Helga," she reports. "She's up and about and says she's well enough to go into town for our little shopping trip. I told her I'd asked you to come along and she seemed very pleased. Are you ready, Isabel?"

It's about half a mile from Moskin's to Harper's Falls along a rutted dirt road studded with stones and tree roots. Most of the guests at Shady Pines walk to town, but because of Helga's wounded ankle, her uncle will drive the four of us in. As I soon learn, my mother is coming along, too. The only good thing about that is that maybe, maybe, she'll buy me the pair of dungarees that I've been yearning for.

As soon as we are in town, it's pretty noticeable that

the war has come to Harper's Falls and changed it from a sleepy country village to a place of bustling activity. Banners in support of the war effort are flung across Main Street, and there is now a Red Cross center and a blood bank. Even the sleepy old railroad depot behind the five-and-ten seems to have come alive with announcements of extra trains daily.

We're dropped off at the town's so-called "department store," which is really just a single-story building, nothing at all like Macy's or the other *real* department stores in New York City with their elevators and escalators to take shoppers to the upper floors filled with endless amounts of merchandise.

"Dungarees, hmm?" says the salesperson who I've rushed to approach as we walk in the door. She's a short, stocky country woman, probably the wife of the owner. "We had a few pairs back in the spring. Might be some left. But there's not much of a choice of sizes."

"What's this all about?" my mother wants to know, as the saleswoman goes off to check the stockroom.

"Nothing, nothing," I reply. "They probably don't have any." I figure there's no use getting into an argument over something that may not exist. Meantime, Mrs. F. has led Helga over to the resort clothing to look at playsuits, halters, shorts, slacks, and cotton skirts.

Helga hops around on one leg inspecting the garments that her aunt takes off the counter or the rack to suggest to her. "Such bright colors," Helga murmurs.

"Exactly," says Mrs. F. "We don't have to hide ourselves in camouflage here in America. You're safe here, Helga, safe at last. But keep in mind that the selection will get smaller and smaller as the war goes on and there will be shortages of material, even of buttons and zippers, of everything."

"That's true," says the saleswoman who went to search for my dungarees. "Buy now. Our stock of everything is running low." She's holding something made of dark blue cloth folded up under her arm, and I reach out to touch it.

"Oh yes." She turns. "Only this one pair left. It's a small size, though."

"What are those?" Helga wants to know, as I grab the dungarees and head toward the curtained-off fitting room just across the floor. My mother is there even before I've gotten out of my shorts. I start pulling the stiff, coarse blue denim pants up my legs. They're fine until I try getting them over my backside.

"What on earth…" My mother is standing there with one hand under her chin and her lips pursed. "Are you crazy, Isabel? You'll tear them. There is no way you can get into them, much less zip them up. Take those things off this minute."

I don't answer her. I'm too busy tugging away. But I know it's hopeless. Even if I got the pants zipped up, my mother wouldn't buy them for me. And if I could somehow buy them myself, she wouldn't let me wear them.

The minute the dungarees have dropped to the floor, my mother is off to give them back to the saleswoman. Why, oh why, couldn't the store have had them even one size bigger? I take my time putting my shorts back on and, just as I'm about to leave the fitting room, the curtain flutters and Helga comes hopping in, the dungarees slung over her shoulder.

"I'm not talking to you," I mumble to my mother as we follow Helga and Mrs. F. out of the store. They are carrying a number of purchases for Helga including, of course, the dungarees that I couldn't fit into. "You had no business giving them to *her*."

"I didn't," my mother protests. "When she saw me carrying them, she asked if she could try them on. What was I supposed to say? Why are you holding such a grudge against that poor girl? What did she ever do to you?"

I take a vow of silence where my mother is concerned and we spend the rest of the afternoon traipsing around town. Mr. F. joins us and goes to the blood bank to donate blood for the troops. Mrs. F. and my mother go into a yarn store and buy olive-colored wool to knit scarves and mittens and socks for the soldiers. Mrs. F. also buys extra knitting needles and promises to teach me to knit as soon as we get back to Moskin's.

My mother suggests we get some supplies from the Red Cross for making up first-aid kits. We'll roll bandages and stuff during our vacation at Shady Pines and then return the kits when they're ready for use in case of an enemy attack at home or on the front lines. Finally we get into Mr. F.'s car with all our packages and head back to Moskin's.

For the rest of the afternoon, Mrs. F. and I sit under a tree and she teaches me how to cast the yarn onto my two long knitting needles and how to knit and purl, the two basic stitches. I'm making, Mrs. F. tells me, a scarf for some G.I., a soldier in the U.S. Army, who will one of these days invade Europe and take it back from Hitler and the Nazis, who have been grabbing everything they can from Russia to France.

With all the stitches I'm dropping and all the help I need from Mrs. F., it's just as well that an invasion of Europe is going to take a couple of years at least. I'm terrible at the "womanly arts" and I'm afraid it's going to be a very long war.

Meantime, my mother and some of the other ladies are sitting nearby rolling bandages for the Red Cross. Helga, after her shopping spree in Harper's Falls, has of course been sent to our room to rest.

"Helga, Helga, *psst*."

It's late that night and I'm dreaming of an endless

skein of olive-colored wool that is threatening to strangle me, when my sleep is pierced by a soft whistle-like sound. I have no idea what time it is, only that it's dark out and that I seem to have been asleep for hours. As I toss over onto my right side, I hear the sound again, followed quickly by an almost inaudible "*Shh.*"

Something is going on, and I instantly smother the instinct to jump up and make inquiries.

"Helga, come on out. Can't you?"

It's the first voice again, and it seems to be coming from the window that is almost directly above my head, which looks out onto the pine forest behind the annex.

"*Ach, nein.* It's too dangerous."

Helga's voice is so close that it almost feels as though she's in bed with me. Actually, she must be crouching on the floor just beneath the window between our two beds.

"Then I'll come in. Is she fast asleep? Is the door open?"

"*Nein, nein,* you cannot. Wait, I come out. I meet you in the back."

I don't dare move. I can hear Helga softly rustling into some sort of garment and tiptoeing out the front door, which she gently closes.

There's only a narrow thorny space between the back of the annex and the pinewoods, where Roy has somehow managed to get to our window. Where will

45

they go now…will Helga join him near the window or will they go deeper into the forest? Or do they have some other place for a rendezvous?

My heart is pounding as I crawl out of bed, listening for the sound of their voices. I peer out the rear window… nothing. I even open the door a crack. No one is in sight. Perhaps I was only dreaming that Helga left our room in the middle of the night to be with Roy. But I give Helga's bed a poke and sure enough, it's empty.

Time passes. I'm so flustered at catching Helga playing Juliet to Roy's Romeo that I don't know how I feel about my discovery. In one way it's exciting…a mystery. She's only known him one day and already there's a certain intimacy between them. What has drawn them together so strongly that he would sneak back to Moskin's in the dark to be with her?

But while I'm looking for answers, I'm also having envious thoughts toward Helga. I'm even going so far as to wonder if I'm going to tell on her. Does she have to have everything…a great figure, stunning hair and eyes, the concern and sympathy of all the guests at Moskin's, tossed kisses from Harry the waiter and hot-eyed stares from the busboys, my dungarees, and Roy?

I get back into bed and crawl under the covers, keeping my ears open for Helga's return. I've decided I'll play dead when she comes back and see if I can read any signs of what's going on when I see her in the morning.

Did I fall asleep again? I must have. Because the next thing I know I'm awakened by a funny squeaking sound. There are tiny animals, field mice especially, that easily find their way into the rooms at Moskin's.

I sit up in bed and reach for the fly swatter that hangs on a hook above me. It's still completely dark out. How am I going to shoo the creature out, whatever it is, without knowing where it is? I'm just about to reach for the flashlight under my pillow, when I hear the squeaking again. This time, though, it's followed by a sniffle. *Squeak…sniffle. Squeak…sniffle. Squeak…sniffle.* There's a rhythm that isn't exactly mouse-like.

I get out of bed, pad across the short distance to Helga's bed, and give it a poke, like the last time, but maybe just a little bit harder.

There's a shriek. Helga sits up in bed.

"Oh," I gasp. "It's you."

Helga's voice is throaty. "*Ach*, Isabel, I'm sorry if I've waked you."

I can tell for sure now that she's been crying or at least weeping.

"Waked me. Well, not exactly. Um, is anything wrong?"

Helga's long hair is tangled around her face and chest. I can see that much in the dark. And her face is pale. "Only my leg aches a bit," she explains. "I went to

47

the bathhouse to bathe it with cool water. And also," she adds, "to use the toilet."

*Aha*, I think to myself. So that's where Helga and Roy had their romantic rendezvous tonight, in the rough wooden building that is used by the annex guests. In a flash I can see them standing together in the damp-smelling shower room with its handful of stalls and its slimy floor and walls. If that's really where they hid out during Roy's visit, that's pretty pathetic.

On the other hand, I'm burning with curiosity. Did they just sit on the flimsy wooden stools and talk to each other? Did Roy hold Helga's hand and stroke her face? Did he embrace her; did he kiss her? Was Helga already crying when they parted?

Will I ever know? When I look down at Helga again, she's thrown her head back on the pillow, one arm is flung across her face, and she's as silent as if she's fallen into a deep sleep.

# Five

Every morning after breakfast, my father and some of the other male guests at Moskin's walk into Harper's Falls to pick up their newspapers, so they can keep up with the war news. They call this exercise their "constitutional." Afterwards they return to Moskin's and sit on the porch all morning discussing the latest reports and chewing on their cold cigar butts from the night before.

I'm sitting nearby struggling with my knitting because it's too cool to go for a swim this early. "Leave it to the Marines," my father rumbles with an air of authority, as he rustles his newspaper. "Those boys finally held off a Jap ground attack on Guadalcanal. They don't come any tougher than that."

One of my dad's cronies reminds him that the Japanese are still way ahead of the game. "So what? Have you any idea how many American prisoners of war they've taken? And what about those Jap air attacks and those Jap submarines in the Pacific?"

"Aahh." My father waves his stale cigar in the air. "That's the kind of defeatist talk that's bad for the war effort."

It's a relief when I see Ruthie approaching on the lawn that slopes up toward the main house of Shady Pines, and I skip down the porch steps to meet her. I honestly don't see how anybody can keep this war straight in their head. There are so many "fronts"...which I guess is why they call it a "World War"...the second one since the first World War. There's the Pacific front where we're fighting the Japanese who attacked Pearl Harbor in Hawaii in December 1941. There's Europe, where Nazi Germany has scooped up one country after another. There's the Russian front, where the Germans are still in a fight to take over Russia and are now waging a big battle at Stalingrad. And there are also German armies fighting in North Africa to keep us from trying to invade southern Europe. I know that much from listening to my father's pronouncements about how important it is to support the war effort (and why I'd better stop whining about having my nose fixed, or else...).

"Where's Helga this morning?" Ruthie wants to know.

It's been a few days now since Helga's midnight rendezvous with Roy, about which I've told Ruthie and only Ruthie.

"Mrs. F. took her into town to have the doctor check on her leg." I'm still carrying my knitting needles and my ball of yarn. I've got about two inches of my soldier's muffler done, but it looks like Swiss cheese and will probably have to be ripped out when Mrs. F. gets back.

"She still hasn't said anything about what happened that night?" Ruthie asks. "Does she ever make any sounds in her sleep?"

"How should I know?" Most of the time, I'm sleeping, too. "But I can tell you for sure that she's mooning over him. And I know he gave her his address in the Navy so she could write to him. She probably will, too, if she hasn't already."

Ruthie sighs. "Well, I think it's pretty romantic…a sort of love-at-first-sight story. Wouldn't you want to have somebody in the war you could write to? You know, just to keep his spirits up? It wouldn't have to be a romantic thing, even…just friendly and supportive. It must be awful for those fellows who are drafted into the Army, being ripped away from home like that."

Ruthie can be such a sob sister, sentimental and even crying real tears about somebody she doesn't even know. I suddenly have a strong impulse to shove my knitting at her, needles first.

"Why would I want to write letters to somebody who didn't even care about me?" I'm not even sure I'd write to my own brother if he was drafted. Well, maybe I would. But only *un très petit peu*.

Speaking of Arnold, guess who's suddenly decided to put in an appearance at Shady Pines for the weekend. When my parents tell me about my brother's unexpected phone call announcing his arrival by train on Saturday morning, I'm sort of surprised. Arnold has been working this summer in a garment factory that converted from making men's trousers to army uniforms, and because of the war effort he even works on Saturdays. He's been saving money for college in the fall and he's such a money hog that I find it strange he'd take off even one day.

But, of course, the thing that strikes me the most about my brother's visit is that here is yet another admirer for Helga. I can already see him taking one look at her and falling head over heels. And what about Helga? How loyal will she be to Roy once she gets a look at Arnold, with his enticing blue eyes and smooth moves?

On Saturday shortly after breakfast, we pile into my father's car to go to Harper's Falls to meet Arnold's train. Ruthie comes, too. She needs to make some bulk food purchases for the hotel and, these days, with gasoline and even rubber tires being rationed, everybody has to be careful not to waste wartime scarcities.

Mrs. Moskin sees us off in her floury white bandana, with last-minute instructions for Ruthie. You'd think we were all going to the moon. I settle into the back seat beside Ruthie and heave a deep sigh.

"What's the matter?" my father inquires. "You sound like the whole world is resting on your shoulders. You don't know how lucky you are to be living in a wonderful democracy like America."

"That's right," my mother chimes in. "When I think of that poor Helga and what she's been through. She doesn't say much, but I can just imagine how terrified she must have been all those years by the Nazis. And from what Harriette Frankfurter tells me, things weren't that much better during those two years in England. They weren't that welcoming to people with German accents. And who were Jewish, no less."

Where, I wonder, is all this coming from? I glance at Ruthie and roll my eyes. All I did was sigh.

"I'm right, Ruthie, aren't I?" my mother says, glancing around briefly.

"Oh yes, Mrs. Brandt," Ruthie replies solemnly.

I give her a killing look. Thankfully, it's only a short drive to the village and we're already there. We still have half an hour until Arnold's train is due so my mother goes off to do some shopping and my father drives Ruthie and me around to the various hotel suppliers who stow the purchases for Shady Pines in the roomy trunk of the Packard. Then we park at the railroad station where my mother joins us with her packages.

"Where did so many soldiers suddenly come from?" my mother wants to know.

It's true. There are young fellows in uniform milling around all over the place, waiting for a train or maybe for transportation by truck to an Army base. Most of them are in newly issued khaki-colored Army privates' uniforms, with sharply folded overseas caps slung through their belts. There are only a few in sailors' whites and, of course, I get a jolt when I see them because they remind me of Roy (who I'm still pretty mad at).

"Yep, the draft is really in full swing these days," my father remarks, rocking back and forth on his heels. "Got to get at those Germans and Japs."

Ruthie and I glance at each other silently. Some of the fellows are really cute in their new uniforms. "Looking for somebody to write letters to?" I tease Ruthie.

Just then there's a long screaming whistle and every-body starts peering down the track. "That'll be Arnold's train for sure," I mutter to Ruthie. "Just watch the way he acts toward me the minute he gets off. He doesn't see me as anything but an annoying kid sister. He treats me like I'm chopped liver."

Ruthie shakes her head. "Maybe he'll be different this time. Why don't you wait and see?" That's Ruthie, always giving the guilty party the benefit of the doubt. Anyhow, she has a slight crush on my brother from summers past.

The train chugs into Harper's Falls in a cloud of black smoke. My father informs us that "it's being pulled by an old coal-fired steam locomotive" and that "the U.S. has got to get itself some new rolling stock if it really expects to win this war." I sometimes wonder why he doesn't just give up his insurance business in New York City and go to Washington to offer himself as a right-hand man to President Roosevelt.

The train is jammed with even more soldiers, their heads popping through the open windows like bunches of flesh-colored balloons. A lot of them get off, a lot of the waiting soldiers get on, an Army truck arrives to pick up the new arrivals and some who've already been waiting around, and finally Arnold's figure swims through the crowd.

He's easy enough to pick out because he's dressed in civilian clothes, a blue shirt and dark trousers. My father and mother rush forward to embrace him. Even though it's been only about a week since we left home for Shady Pines, my parents are hugging Arnold as though they haven't seen him in months.

"So," my mother says playfully after my brother has given me a peck on the cheek and greeted Ruthie rather absentmindedly. "To what do we owe the pleasure of this visit? We did say you should come up for a little rest from work, but so soon?"

"Tell you all about it when we get to the hotel," Arnold says, slinging his overnight bag into the trunk of the car and taking my mother's place in the passenger seat beside my father.

From the back seat where she's sitting directly behind Arnold, my mother leans forward and strokes the back of my brother's head. His hair is the color of dark butterscotch and very thick. "You need a haircut, my darling. Have you been working so hard that you didn't have time to get one?"

Arnold runs his hand over where my mother's has just been. "I'll get one soon. Very short."

"Not too short," my mother cautions with a bossy edge to her voice.

We're back at Moskin's in no time and my father parks outside the kitchen entrance so the busboys can bring in the hotel supplies.

"Come in, come in, everybody," Minnie Moskin beckons. "Arnold made an early train. Surely he didn't have breakfast." She clears one of her well-scrubbed wooden tables and starts to fuss at the stove. Would Arnold like French toast with maple syrup, eggs, cereal, coffee? What about the rest of us? My father says he'll have a little of whatever Arnold is having. Eating a second breakfast at Moskin's never bothers him. My mother and I shake our heads no thanks.

It's so homey sitting here in Mrs. Moskin's kitchen surrounded by all the good smells of her wholesome and generous meals. I keep wondering why my family can't be a happier one. Somebody, it seems, is always being criticized. I, of course, am the worst culprit with my demands for a nose job, for a pair of dungarees, for not appreciating what Helga has been through, and for not doing enough for the war effort.

Arnold, so far, has been told that his visit to us at Moskin's is premature and that he needs a haircut. But then he hasn't even been here an hour.

Mrs. Moskin brings coffee and thick slices of golden, crusty-edged French toast that she makes from leftover loaves of her home-baked bread. "So," my father says, stirring heavy cream into his coffee, "what's doing in the city? How's the job? Is the factory turning out its quota of uniforms? From the looks of all those draftees at the station, they'll soon go into overtime."

Arnold digs into his syrup-drenched French toast. "Not me," he says casually. "I quit the factory yesterday. Figure I'm due for a short vacation. That's why I'm here."

"You *quit!*" my father explodes. "You left your summer job working for the war effort? What kind of an American are you?"

My mother has gotten to her feet. "Now, now, Harold, calm down. I'm sure our son has a good reason for what he did. Don't be so quick to judge."

I remain sitting at the table, keeping an eye on Ruthie who has been lurking off in the distance where she's helping her mother roll out dough for strudel. I'm so glad that for once this isn't about me. It's almost like watching a really good movie.

Arnold, too, is now standing. "Pop, if you'd just give

the other fella a chance to explain once in a while. You're going to be pleased with what I have to tell you. I've joined the Army Air Force. They took me into the *Air Force*. Is that terrific or what?"

My mother sinks immediately into her chair. "You *what*? Oh, my baby. You're not even eighteen yet. You're starting college in the fall. Why did you do that?"

My father pushes his coffee cup away, plants his elbows on the table, and jams his face between his hands. "Crazy. I have a crazy family, crazy children. You couldn't wait for your draft number to come up? Meanwhile you could have started college, maybe—who knows—even gotten a deferment."

Arnold sits down in dismay and, for the first time, he looks at me and something like a spark of shared sympathy passes between us. Then he goes on to explain that ever since last April when the American lieutenant colonel, James Doolittle, led a squadron of fifteen planes off the deck of an aircraft carrier to bomb Tokyo, he's had his heart set on getting into the Air Force.

"Ah," my father retorts. "The Doolittle raids. Do you know how dangerous that was for the pilots of those B-25s? Every one of them could have gone off that carrier straight into the water. It was a cockeyed idea to try to get back at the Japanese for bombing Pearl Harbor. But how much actual damage did it do? Almost nothing compared to the thousands they killed at Pearl Harbor.

You're too young. You're underage. Don't worry, I'll get you out of it. You'll take a rest, like you said, and in a few weeks you'll start college."

But my father is talking to nobody but my mother and me. Arnold has grabbed his overnight bag and dashed out of the hotel kitchen. I have a hunch that already he's on his way to Harper's Falls to board the next train for the city.

"Is everything all right here?" Mrs. Moskin wants to know, as she surveys the ruins of the breakfast she served, plates of half-eaten French toast and cups of cold coffee.

"Yes, yes," my father says, rising from the table. "Perfect. Thank you so much, my dear woman."

I start edging away from my parents to walk over to Ruthie, who's still working on the strudel dough. But I don't get very far. "Isabel," my father roars in a commanding voice. "This way."

# Six

I can't believe how quickly my mother and father and I pack our bags and get into the car to go racing home to the Bronx. Even so, we're too late to catch Arnold at the Harper's Falls railroad station or wherever it is he disappeared to after my father's temper tantrum over his having joined the United States Air Force.

"I honestly don't see why we had to leave in such a terrible rush," I complain from the back seat. Now that Arnold is the one my parents are so mad at, I figure I can take a chance and fuss a little. "I never even had time to say a proper goodbye to Ruthie. Helga and Mrs. F. weren't even back from the doctor's yet. We could at least have waited a few minutes for Mrs. Moskin to make us the sandwiches she offered."

"That's enough, Isabel," my father mutters ominously from behind the wheel. "When will you learn that we are a family...a family in trouble. And we have to stick together."

I don't see our family as sticking together when one-quarter of it has already angrily walked out on us. Nor do

I understand how my super-patriotic father can justify the fact that he doesn't want his own son to fight for his country. Isn't there a word for that? Hypocrite? Two-faced?

"Please don't keep calling Harriette Frankfurter Mrs. F.," my mother chimes in. "It's disrespectful. As for Ruthie and Helga, you can write to both of them."

I don't even bother to answer. I feel really miserable. I know I didn't want to come to Shady Pines and now I'm sorry to leave it, which is stupid. Also, although I should be relieved of the burden of trying to be close friends with Helga, I feel guilty about having walked out on her.

Up front, my parents are now conversing softly with each other. I hear terms like "flat feet," "a punctured ear-drum," "a trick knee," "a hernia."

"Colorblindness!" I offer, leaning forward and in a voice louder than I intended. "If you can't tell red from green, if they both look gray to you, you can't be in the Air Force. I know that for certain. Only I don't think Arnold is…colorblind. So how about a heart murmur?"

"Oh, Isabel!" my mother declares. "What a terrible thing to wish on your brother."

I curl back into my corner. There's never any pleasing my parents. "Well, if you were hoping Arnold would be classified 4-F," I say sulkily, "a heart murmur could have done it. Only it's too late for all that. He's already passed his physical. Remember?"

The closer we get to the city, the hotter the late August weather gets, so we ride with all the car windows wide open and there is too much noise for further conversation. Which is just as well as far as talking to my parents is concerned.

Now that we're on our way home, I'm glad there are only a couple of weeks to go before I can bury myself in school in September...seventh grade at Samuel S. Singleton Junior High. I keep telling myself it will be practically like going to high school because there will be ninth graders roaming the halls, eighth-grade boys who will actually be older than twelve, and I'll be taking intermediate French.

We find a temporary parking space on *Le Grand Concours* not too far from the entrance to our apartment building, and my parents send me into the lobby to try to find Quincy, the porter, to help bring in our suitcases. The heat rising from the sidewalk is stifling and there is also a furnace-like wind that whips old newspapers around my ankles. I'm sure that no boulevard in France looks anywhere as messy as this.

"Why, Miss Izzie, what you doing here?" Quincy greets me with his brilliant smile. "Thought you was in the country, same place as your brother went off to early this mornin'."

I knew this was going to be embarrassing. When you

live in a six-story building with eight apartments on each floor and a genial janitor-porter-handyman like Quincy, everybody knows everybody else's business. At least, I can be sure that Arnold hasn't returned home yet and I can relate that to my parents before Quincy follows me out to the car.

The moment we're inside the apartment, my mother starts dashing around checking on its condition. The stovetop is greasy and has food splashes on it, the sofa cushions haven't been plumped up in the living room, and Arnold hasn't made his bed in the dining alcove where he sleeps.

"Leave a seventeen-year-old boy home alone for a week and look what happens," she complains to my father. "I see now that we never should have gone up to Moskin's this summer. It was a waste of gasoline, wear and tear on the tires, and money. It's time to face it. There's a war on."

"Aah," my father groans despairingly. "You're telling me. What have I been saying all along? But who cares about the stove and the sofa cushions? Where is that boy? Did he run away to the Air Force already? Will he at least come say goodbye to us?"

This is all more than I can bear. It only proves that I was right in the first place. But when I complained about being dragged up to Shady Pines, I was scolded.

"Isabel, where are you going?" my mother wants to

know. "Aren't you even going to unpack?"

"My room is like an oven and you already took my electric fan and put it in the kitchen," I announce. "So I'm going down to Sibby's to see if she's home."

Sybil Simon, better known as Sibby, lives in the building and has been my friend since the start of sixth grade. If only she's back from her beach vacation in the Rockaways, I'll have some place to escape to during the continuing to-do at home over my brother's enlistment.

The Simon's apartment is 2D, at the opposite end of the building from ours, which is 4H, and, happily, Sybil herself answers the door. Her long, freckled face is reddened by the sun, and her tightly curled flaming hair is tinged with gold. She's back from the beach all right, and she looks it.

"What are you doing here?" Her greeting is none too friendly, but that's how she is.

"Who is it?" Sybil's mother calls out from the recesses of the apartment. I like Mrs. Simon. She's a little on the tough side, usually with a cigarette dangling out of her mouth, but really friendly and not "motherish" at all.

We sit down at the kitchen table where Sybil and her mother are having lunch, and Mrs. Simon pours some Coca-Cola for me and offers me a sardine sandwich.

"Aren't you back kind of early from your vacation at the hotel?" Sybil asks. "Everything okay?"

It's no use trying to keep anything a family secret

around here. "Arnold joined the Air Force," I blurt out. "So my father thought we should come home. Uh, to see him off, you know."

"Oh, good thinking," Mrs. Simon remarks, reaching for a cigarette. "You can't do much for the war effort when you're being waited on at a hotel. When does he leave?"

"I don't really know, but I guess it's pretty soon. Um, how is Mr. Simon doing?"

Sybil's father is in the Merchant Marine and he's been ferrying supplies for England across the Atlantic for more than a year now, always at the risk of having his ship torpedoed and sunk by a German submarine. Sybil and her mother don't talk about his job much, but I usually hear the news when her father is expected home on leave.

"Okay, we hope," Mrs. Simon replies, blowing smoke at the open window beside her, which might as well be shut tight for all the coolness it's providing. "Say, why don't you kids go out for a walk. It might be cooler over at the park."

We skip down the two flights of stairs to the lobby. No use taking the elevator and meeting more neighbors to explain things to.

"Your mother seems a little sad," I remark to Sybil once we're out in the street. "Not her usual self."

"Listen," she advises, "don't ask about my dad because

we haven't gotten a letter in a long time. There've been a lot of submarine attacks lately. Everything is hush-hush, so we can't get any information. You know what they say...*loose lips sink ships*. Anyhow, my mom is pretty nervous about how badly things are going with the war. So she's decided to get herself a defense job."

"You're kidding. She's going to work? Who's going to take care of you and...and the apartment?"

"Honestly, Isabel, you're so behind the times. First of all I'm old enough to take care of myself. And the apartment...phooey. It's not fancy with plush sofas and carved polished wood and mirrors all over the place."

I know Sibby is talking about us in 4H but I let that go by. "So what kind of defense job is your mom going to do?"

"Work in the Navy Yard, probably. With most of the men on the front lines, more and more women will be doing stuff like that."

"Your mom's going to build ships?"

"Don't laugh. She can learn to be a riveter or a welder just like any man. Wear goggles and a hard hat, get up on a ladder. Why not?"

I smother a giggle. "Your mom, maybe. Not mine."

"Well, everybody's different." Sibby sighs and there's a pause. "Meet anybody interesting up at that hotel?"

By now we've reached the park and are dangling our bare feet in the fountain filled with slimy green water.

I think a minute and then decide why not. "Yes," I tell Sibby, "a very cute sailor who just enlisted in the Navy and a kind of dreamy mysterious fourteen-year-old refugee girl from Germany. They met each other and they fell in love all in one day."

"Oh," Sybil gasps, kicking her feet rapidly up and down and splashing some of the green slime on both of us, "a love story. I just love a love story. Tell me every-thing."

Even though I've got my electric fan back, I'm lying in a pool of perspiration in my bedroom in the apartment. It must be two or three in the morning at least, total blackness coming from the open window and the air outside warm and perfectly still.

"Hey, Iz!" It's a hushed male voice and I know instantly that it isn't Roy, the indifferent sailor who turned his back on me.

"Arnold," I creak hoarsely, "what are you doing here? When did you get back?" From what I can see of my brother in the door, he is fully dressed in the same clothes he was wearing when he went dashing out of the kitchen at Moskin's about fourteen hours ago.

"I could ask you the same question," Arnold whispers slightly out of breath. "Except you guys seem to have beat me to it. I tried to hitch a ride back to the city and got stuck a couple of times. What's going on with *them*?"

I clear my throat. "Um, our parents? Pop had a fit after you ran out. So we packed up fast and drove home. Mom's upset that you left the apartment in a mess."

Arnold shoves me over and sits down on the edge of my bed. He wipes his brow. "That's what they're having a fit about?"

"No, stupid. It's the same thing as this morning. They want you to be a real patriot like Pop, but not be in the war...somehow. I'm not sure how. I guess you passed your physical already, huh?"

"Well, of course. I report for duty next week."

Suddenly my ceiling light flashes on and Arnold and I are revealed as a pair of middle-of-the-night conspirators. My father is standing at the door in his striped pajamas and my mother is right behind him in her piqué negligee.

"Aha," my father says in a somber voice, "the prodigal son returns."

I don't know what that means but it doesn't sound good.

Meantime my mother has snaked her way around my father and rushed over to get a closer look at her son. "You look terrible, Arnold. Where have you been? How could you have run out on us like that? We went to look for you at the station in Harper's Falls, but you weren't there."

"I got a lift out of town right away," Arnold mumbles. "But the truck broke down. It's a long story."

"You took quite a chance, young man," my father comments, "driving around the countryside with strangers." By this time we're all gathered in the kitchen and my mother is fixing some food for Arnold while he goes off to take a shower. I can't see where hitchhiking is any more dangerous than flying a B-25 bomber, but I know better than to say anything.

We're still sitting around the kitchen table when the first birds begin to twitter in the trees below our windows. My mother hasn't said a word about Arnold leaving the kitchen messy or his bed unmade during the week we were at Shady Pines. My father is planning to drive Arnold to the assembly center next Thursday. That's where his unit is scheduled to meet the bus that will take the inductees to a basic training camp…no one knows where.

I examine my brother's face and notice with surprise that there are faint hollows in his cheeks and tiny wrinkles at the corners of his eyes. Of course, he's had a rough trip home and was on the road for hours. But it's more than that. He's seventeen going on eighteen and he doesn't have as much of a baby face as he did at the start of the summer.

I then realize with a pang that Arnold will be leaving us in less than a week. So I guess that, after all, we're a family like lots of others these days. In the immortal words of my father, we're *a family in trouble*. And because of that, we've got to try harder than ever to stick together.

# Seven

When Thursday comes, we all get up at the crack of dawn, even though it's been agreed that my mother and I won't be going along to see Arnold off at the assembly center. Actually, the meeting place is just one of the big public buildings on the Concourse that has a nearby subway stop for those who are arriving by train. And Arnold could easily get there by himself.

Arnold has a small suitcase packed with extra underwear and toiletries like shaving cream and toothpaste, hair gloss and toenail clippers. My mother is still adding things bit by bit even as he's getting ready to walk out the door—Alka Seltzer and Kaopectate, corn plasters and Mercurochrome.

"I don't see why you're sending along all that stuff," I tell her when Arnold and my father are out of hearing distance. "The other fellows are going to think he's a terrible sissy. Besides, the Army will probably give him the same things for free."

"I wouldn't count on it," my mother remarks grimly. "How could they know better than a mother what a young man requires to maintain good health and comfort?"

I sigh and walk over to the window. The weather has changed overnight. There's a fall tang in the air and the clinging dampness of the long summer seems to have vanished.

"Anyhow," I add, "how far away do you think he's going? Probably only to New Jersey. He can buy anything he needs in the PX or in the nearby town on his day off."

"Since when have you become such an expert on the Army?" my father, who has just entered the room, wants to know. He turns to my mother, not waiting for an answer. "I think we should leave in five minutes, Sally. A Thursday morning on the Concourse, there could be traffic. I don't want my boy to be late. This is the Army."

Arnold emerges from the bathroom. He looks pale and there's a film of perspiration on his forehead. I can't help wondering if he's been throwing up. He refused the scrambled eggs our mother offered him for breakfast, and ate only buttered toast. But still…

We all go down in the elevator together, and even at this early hour there are people in the lobby, most of them setting off for work. Quincy is there, too. "Mos' every day now," he tells us, "they is somebody in the buildin' takin' off for the service."

In the few minutes that we're standing on the sidewalk waiting for my father to pull the car in front, a larger knot of people gather. Some, I swear, are just passersby who've spotted Arnold with his suitcase. I wish we'd said our final goodbyes upstairs.

My mother is red-eyed, although I can't see any tears on her cheeks. My father is stern-faced, his jaw set, as he comes toward us to collect my brother. As my mother reluctantly lets go, Arnold turns to me and gives me the tightest hug I've ever received. "Be good, Iz," he whispers, "and hold down the fort. I'm depending on you." I now know from the faintest yet sourish whiff of his breath that my brother has been sick in the bathroom. But I kiss him ferociously somewhere in the vicinity of his ear, and the next moment, I erupt into a fountain of tears.

Even before school begins, you can tell that the entire country is in a wartime frame of mind. The 1942 fall fashions in the shop windows that Sibby and I examine on our leisurely early September afternoons are full of "victory" clothes. The new suit trousers for men have no cuffs, and the lapels on the jackets are much narrower. All this, of course, is to save woolen and cotton cloth for Army uniforms and blankets.

"And the skirts!" Sibby exclaims. "Short and getting shorter…above the knee. What are girls with fat legs like Sue Ellen Porter going to look like?"

"No pleats," I notice. "And no ruffles. Skirts and even dresses look like two hankies sewn together, same thing front and back. Girdles! We'll soon have to start wearing rubber girdles like Harriette Frankfurter and my mother. Mrs. F., you remember, the aunt of that girl Helga."

"Uh-uh," Sibby cautions. "Positively no girdles. Remember the rubber drive that started back in June? It's still on, you know."

I glance at Sibby's carrot-colored freckles, which probably won't fade until the late snows of winter—and then not much. "You're right."

Back in June, President Franklin Delano Roosevelt got on the radio and said to the American people, "I want to talk to you about rubber." Seems that right after Pearl Harbor, the Japanese took over important Pacific islands where rubber trees grow, so the U.S. started making long-term plans to manufacture fake—well, artificial—rubber. Meantime, the country needed scrap rubber and there was this huge drive—old tires and garden hoses, rubber raincoats and galoshes, rubber gloves and bathing caps. You could take the stuff to the local gas station and get a penny a pound for it.

Kids all around the country started collecting rubber bands and looping them tightly over one another to make rubber balls, as big and heavy as possible. Sibby and I were working on one, too, but had run out of rubber bands. We were also making balls out of tinfoil from chewing gum wrappers. They were supposed to help with the scrap metal drive. I could see melting down old aluminum pots and pans, everything from double boilers to turkey roasters to help build an airplane for Arnold to fly for the Air Force. But tinfoil…really.

After a while, Sibby and I get tired of window-shopping and climb up one hilly street and down another toward home. The war might mean shorter skirts and even the possibility of two-piece bathing suits come next summer, but it's not really a bright side.

My parents and I still haven't heard from Arnold. He seems to have vanished into thin air. Sibby and her mother still haven't had a letter from her father in the Merchant Marine. And even the post cards I've sent to Ruthie and Helga up at Shady Pines, apologizing for our sudden departure, haven't earned a reply.

"*Je souffre*," I tell Sibby as I follow her into the dark-ened lobby of our building, "*d'un grand malaise*."

She whirls around and stares at me. "*Malaise, malaise*. What's *that* supposed to mean? Honestly, Izzie, you are so dramatic. Do you always have to suffer in French? Can't you just say what you feel in English?"

I scowl back at my closest friend (for the time being). "There is no word in English for *malaise*. It's sadder than sad and yet, as Miss Le Vigne says, it's very vague, like an 'enveloping mist'."

Sibby turns her head and starts up the stairs to her apartment on the second floor. "Forget about Miss Le Vigne. Sixth grade is over, remember? I'll see you in junior high next Monday. *If* you can come down from your high horse by then, *Mademoiselle*."

It's scary, but a huge relief to be setting off for our first day at Samuel S. Singleton Junior High School in the Bronx on a rainy September morning. Sybil is over her "mad" at me for being what she calls "a French-speaking snob" and I'm being careful to keep my lip zipped when it comes to using *la langue*.

Besides, there's so much else to think about. Kids who already go to Singleton make fun of it by calling it "Simpleton." But it's still a big step up from elementary school and a lot more complicated. Even though each class will have a home-room teacher, we'll march off to different classrooms for all our subjects. Sibby and I may see each other only a few times during the day. We may not even have the same lunch hour. I'll have to make new friends and get used to five or six new teachers.

The first thing that happens is that we find out our home-room teacher is a man, Mr. Jeffers. He's tall and skinny with poppy eyes and pale skin, a little strange, but he seems harmless. Sybil and I have never had a male teacher, so this is quite a shock. "What," she whispers to me, across our desks, "if we have a sanitary-napkin problem?"

I know she's referring to Miss Haverford in sixth grade, who kept sanitary materials in her supply closet, especially for girls who got their first period while they were in school. No embarrassing trips to the school nurse while the whole class was watching.

"How old do you think he is?" I ponder softly. "If he's between eighteen and thirty-five he's draft age. So what's he doing here?"

"4-F? He's pretty pasty-faced."

"Young ladies," Mr. Jeffers calls out with surprising authority. Sybil and I button up and we stay that way.

Sure enough, it turns out we don't have the same lunch hour. Who knows why schools do those things? Sibby's is early. Mine is late. Maybe it's because of my French class. The first person I see when I enter the cafeteria is Sue Ellen Porter, so I sit down with her and a few other familiars from elementary school. Where are all those new faces from other schools, and those thirteen- and fourteen-year-old eighth and ninth graders I've been hoping for?

Sue Ellen, although she has a pretty face with perfect baby-doll features, has gotten even more blubbery over the summer. So I don't think it's a good idea to open the conversation by asking her what she thinks of the new short "victory" skirts and the prospect of two-piece bathing suits.

I slip my tray down next to hers and blurt out rather abruptly, "My brother just went into the Air Force."

"Oh," says Sue Ellen, her china-blue eyes misting

over, "mine is in the Marines. How long do you think this awful war will last?"

It's been a confusing day—so many teachers that I can hardly keep them apart except for Mr. Jeffers with his library-paste complexion and black panda eyes. And I haven't even had my intermediate French class yet because it only meets twice a week.

"Isabel, I'm on the phone," my mother calls out in a warning voice as she hears the door into the foyer click shut.

Automatically, I tiptoe past the hall table where my mother is seated and head for my room, dump my new school books on the bed, curl over onto my side, and vigorously bicycle my knees into the air in an attempt to push away the past six hours.

"Terrible, oh terrible," I hear my mother muttering into the phone. "When did the pain begin? You must have been beside yourself. Do you really trust this doctor to do the surgery? Six to eight weeks of recovery time. You poor thing. You know, of course, that I'll do anything I can to help…"

I've begun to pay attention to my mother's conversation. This can't be about Arnold. Her tone would be entirely different if anything had happened to my brother. It sounds more like one of her women friends. They're always having operations, it seems, for one disastrous-sounding thing or another—dropped wombs, weak bladders, bleeding fibroids—mysterious ailments known as "women's troubles."

I begin to hover around the telephone because I want to complain about my weird home-room teacher, the horse-faced gym teacher who won't let us do tumbling, French class only two times a week, and not having lunch hour with Sybil.

But my mother keeps shaking her head and waving me away. "You know I would do that for you," she says into the phone, nodding decisively. "No, it's not too much trouble and it can go on as long as it needs to. Of course, it will be fine with Harold. Look, there's a war on. We all have to do what we can for each other. Don't give it another thought. Tonight, tomorrow, whatever is good for you. I'll talk to you later and we'll make final arrangements. Take care of yourself and don't worry. Yes, I'll tell her. She'll be delighted."

The phone goes firmly back on its cradle and my mother looks up at me with a stern expression.

"What's happening?" I demand. Since those last two brief sentences I feel as though something is crawling on me. "*Who* are you going to tell? *Wh*o will be delighted? Who was that on the phone?"

"Harriette Frankfurter," my mother declares, getting to her feet. "She's seriously ill. Must go to the hospital for a long stay. Helga needs a home for the time she's away.

Her uncle travels on business, you know."

"Oh," I say, dragging myself across the hall into the kitchen. "Helga. I might have known it. She didn't even answer my postcard. That's how much she cares about us. Now she wants to come and live here, forever I suppose."

"She doesn't *want* to do anything of the sort, Isabel. What would you like the Frankfurters to do? Send her back to England or, even better, Germany?" My mother bangs her fist on the white porcelain table and it makes a sickly clanging noise that brings me to my senses.

"Where would she go to school if she lived with us?" I muse. "Would she go to 'Simpleton' Junior High? If they took her in, she'd be a ninth-grader…"

"Well, of course, they'll take her in," my mother replies, ignoring my switch on Singleton. "She's a refugee. She has to be taken care of and offered an education. Isn't that the American way?"

# Eight

Then next afternoon, Harriette Frankfurter is lying in bed in her private room in a Westchester hospital with Helga at her side when my mother and I arrive to pick up Helga and take her home with us. It's been a long trip on a subway train and a bus to where the Frankfurters live, north of New York City in a pretty tree-shaded suburb.

Mrs. F. is both tearful and delighted to see us. Her red hair is freshly dyed and her eyeliner is as crisply drawn as ever. If she is pale and sick, it's hard to tell under her expertly applied makeup. She's wearing a pink satin bed jacket embroidered with baby-blue forget-me-nots and, when I lean over to embrace her, I'm enveloped in the heavenly scent of her cologne.

"No crying, no crying," Mrs. F. says to the sad faces around her bed—Helga, my mother, and me. "I have the best doctors and a private nurse. After this operation, I'll be perfectly fine and we'll have the biggest party you can possibly imagine. I'm already making plans for it."

Nobody seems especially cheered up by this announcement. My mother tells Mrs. F. to simply rest and relax in preparation for the surgery, which is to take place the following day. Helga and I just stare at each other dumbly.

"I guess you got my postcard," I mumble. "We had to leave in a hurry because my brother enlisted in the Air Force. How's your leg?"

Helga glances down at her calf. "*Ja*, it's better. Just a small scar."

I simply *have* to ask her about Roy. "Uh, did you ever see that sailor again? I mean after he brought you back to Shady Pines the morning you were bitten by the dog?"

Helga blinks and looks confused. Does she know that I know she left our room and spent time with him that evening?

"You could write to him and thank him, you know. If you had his address."

"Yes, yes," Helga nods. "He is on a ship now in the Pacific…very far away, in the war with the Japanese. He was my rescuer and now I worry for him."

I can see that Helga is way ahead of me. I try hard to think of something else to talk to her about. "Did you and Ruthie spend much time together after I left?"

"Ah, yes." Helga actually smiles faintly this time. "We became good friends. She teached me the Lindy. I think also it is called the Jitterbug."

"Really?" I can't think of another thing to say to this piece of news. So Ruthie and Helga had become close after my father ordered our immediate departure from Moskin's.

"Now, of course," Helga adds, "the hotel is closed for the winter. Ruth lives in the town, where she goes to school. How beautiful it must be there and in the nearby mountains when the snow comes."

"It snows plenty in the Bronx, too," I tell Helga. "You'll see."

But she doesn't seem to have heard me. My mother and Mrs. F. have started to say their goodbyes, and the tears really do start flowing. I give Mrs. F.—who I've come to like a whole lot—a parting hug, just managing to remain dry-eyed, and we go out into the corridor so she can have some final words with Helga. Then Helga comes out of the room carrying her suitcase and we pad our way to the elevator, walking as silently as the floor nurses in their white spongy-soled shoes.

"Well, where is she?" Sibby wants to know.

It's the next morning and she has been waiting for me in the lobby of our building so we can walk to school together.

"You look awfully dragged down," Sibby adds before I can answer her question. "Is something wrong? Helga didn't come back with you last night?"

I roll my eyes heavenward. "She's up there. But she can't go to school until her uncle, Mr. F., gets here to enroll her. He's her guardian. It seems he has to show all kinds of papers to prove that she's here legally."

We start strolling down the street and Sibby shakes her head knowingly. "Oh, of course. I've heard about that stuff. They don't let foreigners, not even refugees, into the U.S. just like that, especially in wartime. A lot of Jews from Germany and other places can't get into the country at all. A few years ago a whole shipload of people tried to land over here and they were turned away. They went back to Europe and probably all dead by now."

"Really?" This seems pretty shocking to me. But what do I know?

"You should try to learn more about what's been going on in the world," Sibby says sharply. "My mother keeps up with all the news from over there."

"I don't know what you're yelling at me for," I complain. "I'm already in enough trouble because of Helga. She's very hard to be friendly with, even though I've tried to do everything I was supposed to. Guess what happened last night. We got home to the apartment and I thought, for sure, she'd sleep in the dining alcove where Arnold's bed was.

"But, no, the first thing that happens is my parents move Helga into my room. *She'll have more privacy*, my mother says. Well, what about *my* privacy? So now I have to share my bedroom with her. And not just for a short time like at Moskin's, but probably forever and ever. Or, at least until Mrs. F. gets well and Helga can move back to Westchester."

"Oh," Sibby says with mock sympathy, "poor baby. You know what your trouble is, Izzie? You're spoiled, spoiled, spoiled. Actually, I'm very anxious to meet Helga and I just bet I'm going to like her a lot. And my mother wants to meet her, too."

Suddenly the light across the Concourse turns green and I make a dash for the other side. This isn't the shortest route to Singleton Junior High, but I think if I don't get away from my so-called best friend we're going to have an awful fight.

"I just remembered something I have to buy for algebra class," I call out over my shoulder. "See you in home-room."

Sybil just stands there, her hands on her hips. Then she tosses her head and continues walking. I feel that everyone has ganged up on me because of Helga. She and Ruthie have become friends, and Ruthie hasn't even bothered to write to me. Now, without even meeting Helga, Sybil is going over to her side, too.

My parents have been making a fuss over Helga ever since they first met her and they've already started treating her like a princess since she's moved in with us. My mother served flapjacks with real maple syrup for breakfast today. On an ordinary Wednesday morning. Unheard of! There's really nothing left to pray for except a successful operation and a speedy recovery for Mrs. F.

Scully, Deutsch, Marinello, Brody, Boylan, Damore… physical training, algebra, music, English, history, and French, not to mention buxom Mrs. Miller for cooking and skinny Miss Scanlon for sewing.

As I'm following at some distance behind Sybil on my roundabout route to school, I'm trying to memorize the names of my teachers and their subjects in this new "departmental" system. Whoever dreamed up such a mess is probably the same person who gave Simpleton Junior High its nickname. All I know is that if I ever lose my program card, I'll spend the rest of the term wandering around the three echoing floors of the vast stone building like a soul in limbo.

It's midmorning now and I'm climbing the stairs to the first session of my intermediate French class, really excited at last about something in junior high, when I become aware of somebody hustling along at my side and muttering, "Isabel Brandt, what a snob."

I turn and it's Billy Crosby from sixth grade who I haven't thought about in months. After all, why would I? He's just another wise guy twelve-year-old, with glasses and an irritating grin. He seems a mite taller than he did back in June at the end of the school year. But he's always been such a know-it-all.

"Oh, it's you," I say, sounding, I guess, disappointed.

"You coulda said hello Monday or yesterday," Billy remarks. "We're in the same homeroom."

"Sorry," I tell him as I hustle along the third-floor hallway looking for Room 322. "This place is so confusing."

"No it ain't," Billy contradicts. "What room you lookin' for, anyway?"

I've finally spotted 322 and I turn in the doorway, Billy still hovering at my side.

"It's okay," I tell him. "I found it."

There are only a few kids already seated at their desks. I don't know any of them. I slide into an empty desk and Billy takes the one next to me. "What, you're taking intermediate French?" I remember now that Billy was in the special French class that Miss Le Vigne gave in sixth grade. And he wasn't very good at it.

"Yeah. Any law against that?" Those glittering eyeglasses and that everlasting grin are driving me crazy. I can't help thinking that Billy's lips must be curved into a perpetual smile even when he's sleeping.

"Didn't know you cared that much about foreign languages," I comment.

"Shows how much you know," he hisses back at me. "French, in case you forgot, is the language of diplomats. You could be lookin' at the next ambassador to France."

"Fat chance," I snicker under my breath.

Billy is leaning far over toward my desk. "What'd you just say?"

"Nothing, nothing." I'm saved from further explanation by the entrance of our French teacher, Miss Damore.

Forget about weird hollow-eyed Mr. Jeffers in homeroom, forget about horsey Miss Scully in physical training, petite Mrs. Marinello in music, bossy-faced Mrs. Brody in English. Miss Damore is, as they say, a vision of loveliness. Pretty, dark-eyed and dark-haired, with an adorable nose and full lips, she comes into the room practically beaming, as though she's really glad to see us.

She writes her name on the blackboard and asks if anybody can decipher its origin. I instantly raise my hand. "It means 'of love,'" I say with modest pride, "except not in French but maybe in Italian."

"*Très bon*," says Miss Damore. She explains that her family did come from Italy more than a generation ago but that she has been teaching French for many years and hardly speaks Italian, at which point I feel my ankle being kicked under my desk.

But when I glare accusingly at Billy Crosby, he's staring straight ahead and I can't imagine how his foot could have reached that far.

Miss Damore gently informs us that, as this is an intermediate French class, we'll be starting out with a review so that she can be sure the seventh- and eighth-graders will be able to keep up. "Who knows," she adds teasingly, "if we're good enough we may even get to the subjunctive later this year."

I cast my eyes down and smile. No way will Billy Crosby be able to "keep up." Not in a million years, if we're going for the subjunctive in French.

After forty-five minutes of Miss Damore, the world is a lovelier place. Horseface in P.T. doesn't see me sneak in a whole series of forward and backward rolls while she's putting out the rest of the mats. At lunch, Sue Ellen Porter and I sit with some eighth-grade girls that Sue Ellen knows from the pool where she swam last summer. And, in English class this afternoon, Mrs. Brody assigns a composition (only she calls it an essay) on the war and how it's changed our lives.

I can certainly do that. In just the last few months, the war has come closer than ever. In my very own home, Arnold has been replaced with Helga.

Even though it's been a pretty good day, it's a relief to return to home-room, rearrange our lockers, and get ready for dismissal. Mr. Jeffers is pacing up and back at the front of the room with his long-legged stride, waiting for everyone to settle down because he usually has end-of-the-day messages for us.

Sibby acknowledges me with a hunch of her shoulder and a blank expression. I don't know whether we're still on friendly terms or what. Also, I see now that Billy Crosby is seated behind me and to my left. I turn around. There's that silly grin again and, I could swear, a wink. Or maybe it was just the light glinting off the right lens of his eyeglasses.

A horrible thought seizes me. Suppose, just suppose, he likes me. I was sure I saw his eyes lingering on my chest when we were walking alongside each other looking for Room 322. Ugh, what a disaster. Suppose a boy does decide he likes you, and you don't like him...*at all*. How do you get him to un-like you?

"Uh-hmm, class." It's Mr. Jeffers getting ready to say something. He always starts by clearing his throat loudly. Then he walks across the front of the room and opens the door to admit someone who appears to have been waiting out in the hall. It's our assistant principal, Mr. Lockhart, a short, dapper man with clipped gray hair, who is leading by the hand none other than Helga.

A wave of absolute silence sweeps across the room. Mr. Lockhart steps forward and says, "Class, I'd like to present to you a new student who has just entered our school. She is from Europe, actually from Germany, where she was born and grew up. So English, especially spelling and writing, may still be a problem for her. Therefore, we will start her off here at Singleton in a seventh-grade home-room.

"Please give her a warm welcome. I introduce to you, Helga Frankfurter."

The silence that has held throughout Mr. Lockhart's brief speech is broken by applause, whistles, and somewhere from the back of the room a deep-voiced utterance of the chilling salute that loyal Nazis offer to Hitler himself: "*Sieg Heil!*"

# Nine

We're out in the schoolyard with a cluster of other kids from our home-room, and Sibby is angrily pummeling the chest of a big kid named Danny Brill with her small freckled fists. Danny just stands there and grins. He doesn't even bother to back away. Sibby's fists might just as well be a pair of fleas.

"Why did you say *Sieg Heil* and give the Nazi salute? Why did you *do* that? *How* could you do that?"

Danny Brill has already received a reprimand from Mr. Lockhart while we were all still in the classroom.

"Now, now, young man, we'll have none of that."

But somehow Mr. Lockhart hasn't ordered Danny to the principal's office, or said what would happen to him if he ever tried any Nazi shenanigans again.

"Do you even *know* what *Sieg Heil* means?" Sybil demands. "It means 'victory for Hitler,' who wants to kill the Jews and all his enemies so he can take over the world."

"Gee," Danny says helplessly. "I only saw it in a movie. It was some kind of a German thing. I don't know what you're gettin' so upset about."

"Aahh," Sibby groans, turning away disgustedly. "You're nothing but an ignorant slob."

Danny likewise turns his back and goes galumphing off with some of his friends. They laugh and hunch their shoulders, and one of them calls back at Sibby, "Hey, Red, don't look now but your pants are on fire!"

Because of the scuffle between Sibby and Danny Brill, I haven't had a chance yet to introduce Helga, who by the way has retreated toward the playground fence, as though she wasn't even the reason for the fray. Which has kept me tracking Helga like a nervous puppy dog, while keeping one eye trained on Sibby.

Suppose Danny took it into his head to punch Sibby back. I couldn't let her fight Helga's battle alone because, even though she started the fight, Helga is my responsibility. So it isn't until Danny and his gang have disappeared through the playground gate that I am able to bring them together and say, "Sybil this is Helga, Helga this is Sybil."

Sybil enthusiastically grabs both of Helga's hands, which have been hanging limply at her side. "I'm so glad to meet you after hearing so much about you from Izzie. Well, um, a lot anyway. Gosh, what you must think of us here in America. First that stupid Mr. Lockhart puts you in seventh grade and then that ape, Danny, yells out those disgusting words in German."

Lila Perl

"*Ach*, it's no matter. I am happy to meet you, too."

"What do you mean it's no matter?" Sibby asks in a peppery tone. "It certainly does matter. Both things matter…a lot. You've got to learn that here in the U.S. we fight for our rights. And there's no Gestapo, no secret police, no marching Storm Troopers to shut us up."

Helga has withdrawn one of her hands to brush a long lock of hair from her cheek. "I think it is better that we do not speak of these things."

Sibby instantly frees Helga's other hand, and we all head toward home in an embarrassed silence. Sibby and I only talk to point out various landmarks so that Helga can find her way without us if she has to. I can't imagine that they will keep her in seventh grade at Singleton for more than a few weeks. Helga is fourteen and she should be in ninth grade.

At the apartment, my mother is waiting impatiently for Helga so that they can set off for the hospital to visit Mrs. F. who is still pretty weak following her operation, which is said to have lasted six hours.

As soon as they're gone, I'm down at Sibby's, where Mrs. Simon has just come off the early shift of her new job at the shipyard. She is wearing overalls, a bandana that covers her hair, and heavy men's work shoes. Mrs. Simon looks tired and her voice is hoarse from yelling, she says, over the noise from the machinery. But she still sets out milk and gingersnaps for Sibby and me, and sits down at the table with us, her head in her arms.

"So," I say to Sibby. "do you see what I mean about Helga? She's very hard to talk to. If you say one wrong thing she shuts up like a clam. And you never know what that's going to be until you say it. Then it's too late."

Sibby sips her milk, crunches on her gingersnaps, and nods. "Something terrible happened to her. You have to find out what it is, Isabel."

"Me? All I ever do is get into trouble over her. Don't ask me to interfere."

Mrs. Simon lifts her head from the table. "All right. Tell me what happened."

We give her a rundown of the events at school this afternoon and the way Helga reacted when Sibby tried to stand up for her. "She refused to even talk about it," I add. "Did she *want* to be put in seventh grade with a lot of twelve-year-olds when she should be in ninth? Was it okay with her that stupid Danny Brill yelled out *Sieg Heil* at her? It's almost as though she *likes* being insulted. That's crazy."

"Let me ask you," says Mrs. Simon, "what do you know about Helga's family in Germany? Are her parents still there? Does she have sisters and brothers?"

"Two sisters, I think. And I know she has letters, written in German…" I stop myself short. I haven't told anybody about that morning at Moskin's when

94

Helga went on a hike and I snooped around among her belongings and found the chocolate box with the picture of the parents and the three little girls, one smaller and the other two older.

"Well," Sibby's mother says, "first of all, you should try to get more information about how Helga managed to leave Germany and be sent to England. My guess is that she was put on one of the Children's Transports. In 1939 the Germans were still letting the Jews leave....*if* some other country would take them. Now, of course..." Mrs. Simon takes the forefinger of her right hand and draws it across her throat, as though she's slashing it with a knife.

Even Sibby gasps and I say, "You mean...?"

"What," says Mrs. Simon, "you never heard the Hitler Youth marching song? It goes all the way back to 1934, the year after Hitler became chancellor of Germany. *And when Jewish blood spurts from the knife, then things will again go well.* Today, nobody gets out alive. If the rest of her family stayed behind in Germany they could be in prison or in a slave labor camp. Or worse."

All this information about what's been going on in Germany is giving me the heebie-jeebies. Why don't we read more about it in the newspapers? All we keep hearing about are the Japs and the war in the Pacific, and that our government is moving the Japanese people who live on the West Coast into camps fenced with barbed wire because they might be spies.

Could it be that some people suspect that maybe Helga is a spy working for the Germans? Was that why Mr. Lockhart and our home-room teacher, Mr. Jeffers, didn't get really angry at Danny Brill's *Sieg Heil*? It's all a mystery to me, wrapped in a tall, silent riddle that goes by the name of Helga Frankfurter.

It's later that evening and I'm doing my homework at the kitchen table when my mother and Helga return from their hospital visit to Mrs. F. My father is out seeing one of his insurance clients, as often happens on weeknights.

"How is Mrs. F…Frankfurter?" I nearly said Mrs. F. My mother would have killed me.

"Not doing well. Very weak," my mother replies, as Helga merely nods a polite hello to me and goes to our room. As soon as Helga is out of hearing, my mother adds, "She looks like death warmed over. Now clear your books off the table so I can put some supper together."

I'm not sure what "death warmed over" means, but I suspect it has something to do with Mrs. F. not having a chance to put on her makeup since the operation.

In the room we now share, Helga is sitting on her bed and reading her program schedule for school tomorrow.

"May I see it?" I ask.

"*Ja*, perhaps you can explain to me what is P.T., what is Alg., what is Eng. comp?"

It turns out that Helga does have ninth-grade classes in physical training and math, while history is eighth grade and English is seventh grade, so her program is a mish-mosh.

I still don't see, though, why they put her in a seventh-grade homeroom. She towers among most of the kids except for a few overgrown brutes like Danny Brill. And, even if she does have a German accent, her English is better than people like Billy Crosby who always says "ain't" and drops all his g's.

"Listen," I say, as my mother calls us in to supper (a macaroni and cheese casserole that's been heating in the oven), "I'm sure things will get straightened out at school and you'll get to feel comfortable there. And I'm really sorry about your aunt being so sick right now."

"Ah, about the school it's no problem," Helga says lightly over her shoulder, "because soon, anyway, I'll return to live with Auntie Harriette."

I purse my lips and don't say a word. My mother didn't seem to have such high hopes for a quick recovery for Mrs. F. but Helga has her mind made up. Can I ever get her to tell me anything about her family, as Sibby's mother suggested? Why does she gloss over everything as if nothing bad ever happened?

I'm chomping away on my gluey cheese-coated macaroni, watching Helga eat hardly anything as usual, when an idea comes to me.

"Helga, maybe you could help me with my homework after dinner. I need some information for my history class tomorrow. It's an assignment about something that happened in Germany a couple of years ago, you know, when you were still living there."

Helga is toying with some string beans on her plate. She looks up. "Ah, Isabel, I no longer studied anything at that time because the government had already burned down the school where the Jewish children were sent. So, you see, I have nothing to tell you."

My mother is gasping with indignation at the Nazis having burned the Jewish children's school. But after learning about the *Jewish blood* song from Mrs. Simon, this afternoon, I'm not surprised. "No, no, you wouldn't have learned about this in school," I assure Helga. "You would know it just by having lived in Germany at that time. It's about the Children's Transports…"

"*Die Kindertransporte*," Helga blurts out in German. Her ordinarily pale complexion takes on an ashen hue and her gray-green eyes grow stormy. "*Nein*, Isabel, it is nothing to talk about."

"But, Helga," I implore, "isn't the…the Kindertransport, the Children's Transport…the way you got from Germany to England? It…well, it probably saved your life. I know it took you away from your family, but…Oh please, couldn't you tell me just a little bit about it?"

My mother, who's been standing over us with two small glass dishes of chocolate pudding topped with dabs of whipped cream, puts our desserts in front of us and sits down beside Helga. She places her arm around Helga's shoulders.

"Now, Helga dear, I know it's hard for you to talk about some things, but couldn't you maybe help Isabel out with her assignment. She hasn't been getting the greatest marks at school, except in French. And I think it's because she doesn't work hard enough at anything else."

I give my mother a sour look and stare down at my pudding, the only halfway decent thing that's been served at this meal.

Then I glance up at Helga. She looks like a trapped animal but, to my surprise, she actually admits that she was one of the many refugee children who were sent to England between December 1938 and September 1939 to escape the Nazis. "Only from babies to under age seventeen were taken. The rest of my family did not go. Papa was already in a labor camp because he was Jewish. My mother and my two sisters were hiding with relatives who were not Jewish."

"But they must have written to you?" I ask hesitantly. I can never admit that I've seen those letters in German that Helga keeps in her chocolate box.

"*Ja, Mutti*, my mother, wrote for a time after the war broke out, and she and my sisters escaped to Holland.

Nothing at all from Papa. And *Mutti* had nothing to tell about him. In May 1940, the Nazis took over Holland. I remained in England two more years, but no more letters came after that. Never."

Helga stops and looks away. I'm afraid this is all she's going to tell me. But then she gulps and says, "Please, Isabel, about the transport, I can only tell you that *Mutti* went with me to the train station. It was September 1, 1939. There were so many children, boys and girls, from orphanages, from broken families, some older children who took care of the babies. *Mutti* said, *Soon we will all come to England and be together again.*

"Then *Achtung!* The train whistle blew. We were pushed into the railway cars like rabbits. Some of the children did not smell so nice. Some were frightened and they soiled themselves. We rode for a long time all the way to Holland where we were taken to the port and put on a ferry. Then many more *Kinder* got sick from the movement of the boat in rough waters. At last we arrived in the English port, a place called Harwich."

I've been picturing the awful voyage that Helga made and I'm happy to hear that it finally ended. "What a relief it must have been when you arrived on dry land."

My mother, too, has been listening with bated breath. "You poor child. Your Aunt Harriette never said anything about how you traveled from Germany to England. I'm sure the English people were very nice to you and made you feel at home. Didn't that help even a little bit?"

Helga stands up. She hasn't touched her chocolate pudding. "I will go to my room now, please. Isabel, you can write your paper for the history class. I hope it gives you a good grade."

Once Helga is gone, my mother brings her hands to her mouth and shakes her head back and forth. "Harriette is afraid that both her parents and even her sisters are all gone by now," she whispers. "Hearing her story is a good lesson for you, Isabel. It should make you realize how fortunate you are."

Why does my mother have to turn *everything* into a criticism of me? I start clearing the dishes off the table. "Excuse me," I say abruptly. "I need to write down Helga's description of the Children's Transport while it's still fresh in my mind. I wonder how you spell the name of that place in England where the ferry finally landed."

# Ten

A few days later, long-awaited letters arrive at last. There is one from Arnold. My father reads it aloud several times with great pride, as if he alone had engineered Arnold's decision to go into the Air Force.

All this time, my brother's been at a Basic Training camp just across the river in New Jersey. In a week or so he'll be coming home on a furlough for two days. Then he'll be shipped out to an unknown destination for special aeronautics courses. He's feeling fine and hopes we are all okay, too.

I remind my mother that I was right when I told her Arnold was probably only going as far as New Jersey. "Isabel," my mother says, "when will you learn to take this war seriously? You can be pretty sure that not long after his furlough your brother will be flying planes over the steaming jungles of the Pacific."

"Not until he's properly trained for it," my father informs her. "Do you think the Army sends our boys up just like that before they've become skilled airmen?"

"Yes, I do," my mother insists. "They need every pilot

they can get. They probably give them a few lessons and off they go to battle it out in the air with the Japanese, who everybody knows are nothing but murderers."

My father opens his newspaper with a sharp, crackling sound to signal his annoyance, and I leave the room so my parents can continue bickering without interruption.

There's also been a letter from Sibby's father, all the way from England. His ship had a rough crossing, pursued by German submarines, so they were forced to alter course and arrived in port way behind schedule. After the return crossing he hopes to have a week or so of home-leave. This is good news for Sibby and her mother.

And *I* have a letter from Ruthie. It appears to be a belated answer to my postcard of weeks ago. Ruthie, of course, has no idea that Helga is now living at our apartment, and I want to read this in private. It's Saturday morning and Helga is in our bedroom, so I say I'm going down to Sybil's and will be right back.

*Dear Izzie*, Ruthie writes, (I'm reading this in the stairwell between our floor and the one below),

*I guess you're mad at me. But don't be. School started and I had to help with closing up the hotel. Now we're all settled in Harper's Falls for the winter. How is your brother? Did he really go into the Air Force?*

*Do you ever see or hear from Helga now that*

she's living with her Aunt and Uncle in Westchester? I guess maybe not, since you weren't too crazy about her. But I wanted to tell you something that happened after you left Shady Pines.

Helga seemed so lonely, so one day I asked her if she wanted to walk over to a nearby farm with me. It's where we buy our chickens and our eggs for the hotel, and my mother wanted me to settle some accounts with them. As soon as Helga saw it was a chicken farm, she got kind of upset and she asked me who ran it. It's an older couple, who've owned it for years. I told her their name but she didn't seem that interested.

Just then she said she was feeling sick and, even though I wasn't going to take long, she turned around and walked back by herself. When I got to the hotel, I asked her if she was okay? She said she was fine. The smell of the place, though, had made her feel like throwing up. And then she added that she never wanted to see another chicken farm in her life! Do you think the Nazis made her work on a chicken farm in Germany?

Did Helga tell you we practiced the Lindy? She was pretty good at it. Do you think she ever heard from that sailor Roy? How is school?

> Write soon,
> Ruthie

Now I really do go down to Sybil's so I can tell her the "chicken farm" story and see what she makes of it. Mrs. Simon is there, too, because today happens to be her day off. She works at the shipyard six days a week on the "early shift" from six in the morning to three in the afternoon.

Since Mr. Simon will be coming home on leave soon, Mrs. Simon is more like her usual vivacious self. She's wearing a bright plaid housecoat, she's manicuring her nails, and her dark eyes glitter. Sibby has just washed her hair and is fluffing out her wet red ringlets.

"Oh, I'm glad you came by, Isabel." Mrs. Simon says. "Sibby and I were just making plans to visit the U.S.O. club later today. I hear that since they opened they're getting more and more young fellows in uniform from all over the country. I thought, well, why not volunteer and try to make them feel at home. Want to come along?"

*USO!* What a terrific idea. I think U.S.O. stands for United Service Organizations. These gathering places for the new recruits are springing up all over the country… in meeting halls and community centers and public buildings, wherever there's a big enough space to serve coffee and doughnuts, to sit and talk, and to set up music for dancing. But will my mother really let me go?

"Say something, Izzie," Sibby urges. "You look… discombobulated."

I snap to attention. "Of course, I want to go. I'm dying

to volunteer. Do you honestly think anybody will dance with us? Oh, and what should we do about Helga?"

"Helga. Of course, Helga," says Mrs. Simon. "It'll give me a chance to meet her at last. How is she doing, by the way?"

I whip Ruthie's letter out of my pocket. "That's what I really came down here to talk about. Something having to do with a chicken farm. I don't know if it makes any sense." And I start reading the part in Ruthie's letter about how Helga turned sick and left after she and Ruthie got to the farm.

"Do you think the Nazis made her work on a chicken farm?" I ask. "We know about her father being put in a labor camp."

Mrs. Simon shakes her head. "Feeding chickens and raking up their muck sounds too easy to me. Nazi labor camps are designed to kill, so that more laborers can be brought in and worked until they drop. It's a slow-murdering process. Did you ever find out, though, what happened to Helga *after* she landed in England with the Children's Transport?"

"Uh-uh. She won't say much about England except what I already heard from her aunt, Mrs. F. I told her I needed more information for my history report. I wanted to know if, after she and the other refugee children arrived at the ferry terminal, did a family choose her and take her to live with them?

"All she would tell me was that, before she came to America, she was living in a youth hostel near a British army base. That was when she was able to contact her uncle, who arranged for her to enter the U.S."

"Ah," says Mrs. Simon, her eyes snapping, "What happened between twelve and fourteen? That's what we've got to find out. Something is bugging that girl and I have a hunch that, whatever it is, it isn't pretty."

"You want to go to a U.S.O. dance with Sybil Simon?" My mother doesn't only sound disbelieving. She sounds outraged.

"But I told you, Mrs. Simon is taking us. She's over thirty-five so she's legally qualified to be a senior hostess. She can take anyone she likes with her. And we're going to ask Helga to come, too."

"Helga's only fourteen and you two are twelve. To be a junior hostess I hear you have to be eighteen. And I think that's a terrible idea. I can just see some ill-fated romance blossoming between an eighteen-year-old girl and one of those homesick young servicemen."

"Well, nothing like that is going to happen with any of us. We're too young and Mrs. Simon is too old."

"And married," my mother says pointedly. "I don't see where that woman gets so much energy. She has one day off a week from her war job and she goes to a U.S.O. dance."

"It's not only a dance," I insist. "We serve food there and see if the fellows need any sewing or mending done, or want help writing a letter home. And think of Helga," I add, lowering my voice. "She's been moping in our bedroom, supposedly doing homework, all afternoon. She never goes anywhere or has any fun. I'm sure Mrs… her Aunt Harriette…would approve. Why don't you call the hospital and ask her?"

My mother doesn't answer or make a move to call Mrs. F., who is still in deep recovery. But the idea of volunteering at the U.S.O. club for Helga's sake seems to turn the tide. Even my father, who's been overhearing our conversation in the living room, while keeping his ear peeled to the radio for the war news, agrees with me.

"Those brave young men certainly deserve everything we can do for them." He turns to my mother. "I'm sure, Sally, that you'd want some nice motherly woman looking after Arnold when he gets shipped out to flight training school in Wyoming or wherever."

"Not really," she replies. "I can mend socks for my own son myself, thank you very much."

The U.S.O. club near *Le Grand Concours* is within walking distance of our building, and it's nothing fancy. Actually it's an empty store that local business people have set up with help from the Salvation Army, the YMCA, and Jewish and Catholic welfare groups.

Inside, it's draped with American flags and big USO letters in red, white, and blue. There's a dance floor and a jukebox. There are small tables and chairs, like in an ice-cream parlor. And there's a food counter for coffee and soda pop, with doughnuts and cookies and some wrapped sandwiches.

Right now, in the early evening of this late September day, there are only a few servicemen and not many volunteers. Helga scans the room, almost as though she expects to see Roy here. But there aren't any sailors here at the moment, and I've found out that she hasn't heard from Roy since his letter informing her that he was in the Pacific.

Helga is wearing the same flowered dress that she wore that first night at Moskin's, and she looks lovely and much older than fourteen, while Sibby and I, even though we're dressed in new fall get-ups, still look like the *petits enfants*—little kids—that we are.

Soon after we're in the door, Sibby's mother decides that the place needs some pepping up and she puts money in the jukebox, which comes to life with the new Hit Parade song "Deep in the Heart of Texas." Immediately, a soldier who's been leaning on the counter drinking a bottle of soda pop asks Mrs. Simon to dance.

In no time, she's up on the floor and dancing a foxtrot to the jazzy tempo. I turn to Sibby. "Your Mom's a great dancer."

"Oh, sure, she used to win all kinds of prizes. Come on, let's you and me try it." The rhythm is infectious and Sybil and I really go at it, doing any old kind of step and pushing and pulling each other around the dance floor until Sibby's face starts turning hot pink.

"Look, look," I point out to Sibby, turning her around hard. "There's Helga. She's dancing, too. With one of the soldiers from that table where four G.I.'s were sitting when we came in. He's a hot dancer, don't you think?"

"Stop, stop," Sibby replies. "This I've got to see."

We get off the dance floor and move to the sidelines, where a few of the other women volunteers are watching Sibby's mother strut her stuff. These women look older and more "housewifely" than Mrs. Simon. Their hair is done up in tight permanent waves and they're wearing aprons to serve coffee and fix food. The expressions on their faces aren't exactly approving. But there aren't any junior hostesses here right now and is it awful for married women, who admittedly could be their mothers, to dance with the boys?

Sibby and I are a lot more interested in Helga and her soldier. He's tall and blond and just a little bit gawky, but they look really good together. The music stops and the next number is a slow one, "I Don't Want to Walk Without You (Baby)."

Helga's soldier asks her to dance again and she does. This time they're actually talking to each other as they whirl around lazily, the only couple on the floor. I wish I knew what Helga was saying to him.

Sibby's mother has quit dancing and is behind the food counter now along with the other ladies, making up fresh ham-and-cheese sandwiches with supplies from the refrigerator.

I pull Sybil over there with me, since I feel pretty stupid just standing around and watching Helga.

"Can we help?"

"You'd better," Mrs. Simon says. "What do you think I brought you kids along with me for?"

Pretty soon we've made up about a dozen sandwiches, smearing margarine on slices of white bread (butter is rationed because of the war) and slapping more cheese than ham between the slices (because meat is rationed, too). I've heard that coffee is going to go on the list of civilian food shortages, but I guess there will always be coffee allotted to the U.S.O. and to the troops.

Helga joins Sibby and me and we start circling the room offering sandwiches as well as doughnuts and coffee to the G.I.'s. More have started to drift in and so have civilian volunteers, including a few junior hostesses, so it's getting pleasantly crowded in the storefront U.S.O.

Helga actually looks happy as she extends the tray of sandwiches across the table where the soldier she danced with is sitting with his three companions. He smiles and winks at her as he reaches up for a sandwich. "Don't forget," he says to Helga, "I'm keepin' my eye on you. You owe me one more dance."

"*Ach, ja,*" Helga says softly. "but not so fast as the first one. Still I am dizzy from this song about the heart of Texas. It must be crazy in that place, but I would like so much to see it."

"Hey," says the soldier sitting beside Helga's dance partner. "Where you from, girlie?"

Helga looks slightly alarmed at the soldier's challenging tone and the roughness of his voice. I'm standing right next to her holding a platter of doughnuts, so I answer for her. "She's from here, just a few blocks away, over on the Concourse. In fact, she lives in my apartment."

"Oh yeah, sister?" The soldier shakes his head from side to side. "Don't tell me no lies. You sound normal. But this one's a *Fräulein.* I know a Kraut when I hear one. What the hell's she doin' dancin' with G.I.s in a U.S.O. club? Lookin' for secret information about the military? *That's* what she's doin', ain't she? She's spying!"

By this time Helga's dancing partner is on his feet, as well as the three other soldiers at the table. It's hard to tell who started throwing punches and slapping heads, and which ones are now trying to wrestle which other ones to the floor. It seems likely, though, that Helga's dancing partner started the fight because of the insulting accusations of his tablemate, probably a guy he hadn't even known until this evening. Anyway, in no time at all it's a big tangle, with other G.I.'s joining in, chairs being turned over, and the ladies in the aprons screaming, "Stop! Stop!"

Mrs. Simon races toward us and starts pulling Helga and Sibby and me away from the brawl. Sandwiches and doughnuts are already on the floor and being trampled and squashed. It's beginning to look like the whole U.S.O. club is about to be trashed, when a shrill whistle sounds and somebody yells, "Police!"

Everybody freezes for an instant and then in come the M.P.s—Military Police—uniformed members of the armed forces who have the power to arrest soldiers who misbehave, riot, go absent without leave, mutiny, or whatever.

Seven or eight soldiers, including the one who danced with Helga, are dragged away and put into a military van that's standing out in front of the U.S.O. Sibby's mother starts cleaning up the mashed food that's on the floor and picking up the chairs that have been toppled over, and she motions to us to do the same.

"Finish up, girls, and let's go," she says hoarsely. "Where are your sweaters and jackets?"

I find mine and Sibby's. I look around for Helga's, which was hanging on the next hook. But it's gone. And so is Helga.

# Eleven

"Stop worrying about her," Mrs. Simon repeats over and over in response to my laments, as we hurry home through the dark, chilly streets. "And for Pete's sake," she adds, "stop calling me Mrs. Simon. My name's Leona."

I've known this for a while because Sibby sometimes calls her mother by her first name. But after being yelled at for saying Mrs. F. instead of Mrs. Frankfurter, I'm forever on my guard.

"I'm sure she headed straight for home and you'll find her at the apartment when you get there," Leona Simon assures me.

I don't happen to agree but we'll find out soon enough.

"What a numbskull that soldier was," Sybil reflects, "to accuse Helga of being a spy. Insulting her by calling her a Kraut would have been enough."

"*Fräulein* I understood," I mumble. "It's German for a 'Miss'. But where does Kraut come from, anyway?"

"Oh, you're so out of it, Izzie. It comes from sauer-kraut. Pickled cabbage. They eat a lot of it in Germany.

Golly, didn't you ever have a hot dog with sauerkraut?"

"Okay," I say huffily. "You don't have to get nasty about it. I just didn't make the connection."

"Stop bickering, girls, and keep your eyes open for her," Leona orders. She's walking faster and faster and we're all looking around for Helga. How much of a head start could she have had? Surely we'll catch up with her before we get to the door of our building.

When we burst through the entrance, I'm happy to see that Quincy is in the lobby. Surely he'll have just seen Helga return and we can all take a deep breath. But, having sensed already what is wrong, Quincy shakes his head sadly. "No'm, Miss Izzie, I ain't seen the young lady this evenin'."

"Come on then, kids," says Leona determinedly. "We'll all go up together and face the music."

It won't be very musical, I think to myself. My mother will be hysterical when we tell her that we lost Helga.

For the first few seconds, my parents receive Leona and Sybil pleasantly. Maybe my mother has been feeling a little sorry about some of her criticisms of Mrs. Simon. But it doesn't take long for both my parents to notice that Helga isn't with us. Nor, of course, has she come home to the apartment.

"What do you *mean* she left the dance early?" my mother demands, addressing her question to me. "How could you let her walk out of there alone, Isabel? It's dark out; she doesn't know the neighborhood."

"I didn't even see her go," I protest. "It wasn't until a couple of minutes later that I realized she had walked out of the place. She never said a word to anyone."

My father has already put on his imitation bomber jacket and declared, "Ladies, stay where you are. I'll find her."

"Oh," my mother exclaims, as he rushes out the door, "how could all *three* of you lose her? What kind of a sense of responsibility is that? Did something happen at the U.S.O.?"

Leona, Sybil and I exchange glances. By silent agreement we know that we aren't going to describe the fight scene that erupted over the words the mean-talking soldier had flung at Helga.

"I know I never should have let Helga go. And not Isabel either," my mother rants on. "Some people take life entirely too lightly."

"Please calm down," Leona advises my mother, realizing that she's now the chief target of my mother's wrath. "I suggest we call the police."

"The police!" my mother screams. "The police. That's all we need...a scandal. No. Thank you for your wonderful suggestion. I think my husband is capable of finding her."

All this time, we've been standing in the foyer

and Leona Simon hasn't even been asked to sit down. Suddenly she brushes past my mother and sashays into the living room, where she takes a seat in one of the puffed-up easy chairs. "I take full responsibility for Helga's safety," Leona declares, "and I intend to remain here until she's accounted for."

Sybil follows her mother, and my mother turns and goes into the kitchen with me trailing behind her.

"It's not our fault," I hiss. "Didn't you ever happen to notice that Helga has a mind of her own? Maybe you should offer Leona a cup of tea. She always treats me to refreshments when I visit Sibby."

"Ah," says my mother. "So now it's Leona. No wonder some grownups who are on a first-name basis with children behave like children themselves."

I'm about to launch into a defense of Leona Simon when we're all startled by a loud banging on the apartment door...no doorbell, no turning of the key... just a fearful pounding with what sounds like a very big fist.

I'm first at the door and, without even taking the usual precaution of looking through the peephole, I fling it wide open.

"Brandt?" It's a burly, red-faced New York City cop, holding by the hand a pale, shrinking Helga. Her shoulders are hunched, her eyes averted, her lightweight coat hangs limply over her flowered dress. She looks—I hate to say it—like one of those cartoon characters that have been flattened into a pancake after being run over by a steamroller.

The moment the police officer lets go of Helga, she dashes away to our bedroom and shuts the door firmly. I look around doubtfully, wondering if I should follow her. I imagine, though, that she has collapsed in a flood of tears and ought to be left alone to work through her shame and terror at having been delivered to our door by a member of the New York City police force. Even though American cops are very different from the Nazi police, I know she's scared stiff of authority figures in uniform.

Instantly, we're all cackling at the policeman, demanding to know where he found Helga and if she's been in any sort of trouble.

"Calm down, ladies," he advises. "She was in the subway station wandering around on the platform, seemed pretty confused. I noticed her watching the trains, kind of nervous and not sure about getting on. I figured her for a runaway."

My mother throws her hands in the air in a wild gesture. "Where could she have been going, and at this time of night? To her Aunt Harriette? Harriette's still in the hospital. She's had a slight relapse. Helga knows that."

A runaway! We're all pretty baffled. I know that Helga isn't happy here with us. She isn't in the right grade in school, and some of the stupid kids in our seventh-grade homeroom have started calling her "Helga Hot Dog."

She wasn't even happy when we were at Shady Pines, except for Roy. And now he's off fighting in Guadalcanal or some other Japanese-infested island in the Pacific. But for Helga to plan on running away? Where would she run to? Would she really do such a thing?

"I'm gonna leave the girl with you, ma'am," the policeman says to my mother. "But let me give you a word of advice. She might be a so-called refugee with the papers to prove it. But she's a German national and we're at war with Germany. Keep close tabs on her. There's talk about spies getting in the country. If she finds herself in the wrong place at the wrong time, she could get into a lot of trouble."

"Well, I never…" my mother begins.

Leona Simon steps forward. "That's good advice. We're really grateful to you, officer."

Sibby and I glance knowingly at each other. Thankfully, nothing has come out about the ruckus at the U.S.O., which was exactly the sort of the thing the policeman was referring to. But I'm still unclear about where Helga was intending to go when she ran down into the local subway station.

My mother is actually serving tea to Leona, and milk and cookies to Sybil and me, when my father's key turns in the lock and he bursts through the door like a charging bull.

"Well, any news? What is this, a tea party? I looked everywhere within a radius of twenty blocks. The girl's lost…lost, abducted, kidnapped into the white slave trade, who knows what! And we're going be held responsible. Herman Frankfurter will never speak to me again. And he'll be right, right, absolutely right…."

All this time, my mother is waving her arms and entreating my father to put a stop to his tirade. "She's here, here, Harold. A police officer found her and brought her home. He left not ten minutes ago. Everything is all right."

My father collapses into a chair. "Well, for crying out loud, why didn't somebody tell me?"

When I go to my room a little later I knock softly on the door first. It isn't really my room now that Helga is sharing it, and I'm always afraid I'll interrupt her or embarrass her—or myself—if I don't behave formally. She's different from somebody like Sibby; I'm sure that if we two roomed together, we would go around stripped to our panties without thinking anything of it. Everything would be, as the French say, *au naturel*.

Helga is still fully dressed, sitting on her bed and looking through some school assignments. She's been working hard on her English grammar. But I wonder how she can study at a time like this.

"*Ach*, Isabel," she says, "I am ready to go now and apologize to your parents for the terrible trouble I caused. I will explain that I came into a panic when the fighting began in the U.S.O. and I could think only that I must run away from it. Perhaps otherwise I would be arrested for being the cause of this trouble…"

Helga is already getting off the bed and putting her shoes on so that she can go into the living room to explain things to my mother and father. She is so proper that heaven forbid she should walk out of here shoeless.

"No!" I hiss at her urgently. "You mustn't say anything about the fight at the U.S.O. You'll only get Sybil's mother in trouble for having taken us there in the first place. Besides, none of that was your fault."

But Helga is stubbornly continuing to fasten the straps on her shoes, when there is a sharp rap at the door and my mother slides into the room.

"Are you two all right in here? How are you feeling, Helga? Will you please promise not to frighten us like that again? It's very dangerous for a young girl to go wandering around on the subway stations at night. Why did you do that?"

I give Helga a warning look. "She panicked," I answer for her as hastily as I can. "It became so crowded at the U.S.O. She couldn't breathe. So she started to walk home without telling us. But she got lost. That's why she went into the subway, to see if she could find a policeman."

My mother frowns at me. "Isabel, would you mind letting Helga tell it herself. She's perfectly capable of doing so. Helga?"

"*Ach*, *ja*, Mrs. Brandt, it's true what Isabel says. It became so hot in that place. I thought I would faint. Only, once out in the street, I became confused and lost my way. So then I thought of the subway station…" Helga's voice has become choked with emotion and it seems for a moment that she is going to cry.

"Now, now, dear." My mother perches on the side of Helga's bed and pats her shoulder. "It's nothing to get upset about. As long as you're back, you know that you're safe here with us. I'm so glad that police officer was wrong when he said that he spotted you as being a runaway."

My mother advises us that she and my father are going to bed. She reminds Helga that she's left milk and cookies for her in the kitchen. Helga and I are alone once more.

To my surprise, Helga undoes the buttons at the back of her dress and lifts it off over her head, something she wouldn't ordinarily do in front of me. Standing there in her slip, she says, "I am a good liar, Isabel, *nein*?"

I'm dumbfounded. Helga's tone is so different from her regular one. There is a bitter ring to her voice and it is more high-pitched than usual. Now I seriously am wondering if Helga is going to become hysterical.

I am sitting cross-legged on my bed, staring at her. "That was only a white lie, Helga. And thank you for backing me up and saving Mrs. Simon from having to take all the blame for what happened tonight."

Helga shakes her head stubbornly. "It was a lie, Isabel. I have told lies before, and one very big lie that I will pay for all my life. I promised myself that after I came to America I would never lie again, not even for the smallest reason. Never! But, you see, now I have done it. And whatever happens to me for this, it does not matter. I deserve it."

Helga grabs her bathrobe and pajamas and runs off to the bathroom. I can't tell whether she is really crying this time or is simply in a frenzy of self-anger. Most baffling of all, what is Helga talking about when she says, *One very big lie that I will pay for all my life?*

# Twelve

"Are you okay, Helga? You don't feel sick or anything?"

A week has gone by, and Helga and I are sitting side-by-side in a subway train that is taking us to the very last stop in New York City. From there we'll get on a bus that will drop us at the hospital in Westchester where Harriette Frankfurter is making a slow recovery from her operation.

Ordinarily, my mother would be with us. But today, she's expecting Arnold to arrive on his furlough and she's busy preparing all the food goodies she can with her limited number of ration coupons. So she's designated me to be Helga's guide because I'm sort of an "old hand" at getting around the city.

Helga seems especially nervous today. Maybe it's because there are so many soldiers and other uniformed men on the trains. Maybe she's worried about meeting the policeman who brought her home last week suspecting that she was a runaway.

Anyhow, I can't help noticing that she keeps her head down most of the time and looks up only when the doors open to admit new passengers, and then very cautiously.

"I still don't understand," I say as gently as I can. "If you don't like the trains, and the people on them scare you, what were you *really* doing in that subway station all by yourself last week?"

Helga shakes her head and I can't even see her eyes. She is wearing one of the khaki-colored caps with a visor that she brought with her from England. "I already explained to you, Isabel, after these lies I tell I don't care what happens to me. If it is something bad, it is my punishment. That one time, when the policeman comes over to me and says where do you live, I tell him. That one time and that time only."

"So," I say, twisting my neck at an uncomfortable angle to try to see Helga's half-hidden face, "you really were planning on running away. But where would you have gone? Would you try it again? You can't do that, Helga. Something terrible could happen to you."

There is a fierceness in Helga's reply. "I already told you what is the reason. It's for me to suffer what happens."

I'm suddenly gripped with the fear that Helga may actually be having thoughts of throwing her life away. All week she's been like this, secretive and talking in riddles that are very scary.

When the train comes to a halt at its final stop at the city line and everybody gets off, I clutch her hand as tightly as I can. I watch her nervously as we wait at the bus station. When the bus comes, I push her on ahead of me and sit beside her until it's time to get off.

"Oh, my darling girls are here!"

Harriette Frankfurter is seated in a chair in a sunny corner of her hospital room. She is wearing a long white silk dressing gown with sequin appliqués of butterflies in delicate but dazzling colors. Her hair and makeup are perfect as usual.

A white-uniformed nurse and Mr. F. are also present. Fresh flowers fill every corner of the room, and a box of sumptuous chocolates lies open on a bedside table.

Helga embraces her aunt. I follow with a gentle hug and am enveloped in Mrs. F.'s lilac-scented cologne. I tell Mrs. F. how well she is looking, and I learn that she'll be going home soon with the private nurse, who's now in the room, to take care of her. Mr. F. looks on approvingly.

"I want a nice long visit this time," Mrs. F. declares. "But first, you girls must be hungry. Uncle Herman will take you down to the coffee shop for lunch."

"Honestly," I say, the palms of my hands encircling my stomach, "I couldn't eat a thing. I had such a big breakfast. But Helga ate almost nothing this morning…"

The plan I've been cooking up for this visit works. Mr. F. goes down to the hospital's coffee shop with Helga, the nurse takes a break from her duties, and I'm alone with Mrs. F.

Why do I get along so much better with other grown married women, like Leona Simon and Mrs. F., than I do with my own mother? The moment we're alone I can see that we're on the same wavelength. Mrs. F. leans forward and her black-rimmed mascara-brushed eyes take on a concerned look.

"Why is Helga wearing that depressing military cap and those awful khakis they gave her at that dreary hostel in England? She has much nicer things. And, please understand that this isn't meant as any sort of criticism, dear, but why does she look so thin and seem so nervous?"

This is just the opening I've been hoping for. I know my mother would kill me for worrying her good friend Harriette Frankfurter with reports about Helga. But I think it would be wrong to hold back. It's important to tell Mrs. F. how Helga's been acting lately, and some of the scary things she's been saying.

So I blab the whole story from *Sieg Heil!* and "Helga Hot Dog" at school to the U.S.O. fight over the soldier who called Helga a Kraut and a spy. I tell Mrs. F. about Helga running away from the dance and being brought home by a policeman who found her in the subway station. I ask her if she knows what Helga means when she talks about deserving to be punished for telling lies. And I ask her if she knows anything about the *one very big lie that I will pay for all my life*.

Mrs. F. listens with a mixture of pity and alarm. "Oh, the poor child. All this after what she went through in England. Did she tell you about her life on the chicken farm and then in the hostel? But lies...telling lies she should be punished for...I don't know about any such thing..."

I pounce at the mention of the chicken farm. "Was that where she lived when she first arrived in England? No, she never told me."

Mrs. F. sighs deeply. "She wants to forget it. It was just very bad luck. Most of the German refugee children are being treated well over there from what we hear. But, you know, when Helga arrived in England she waited a very long time with the rest of the Children's Transport for someone to offer her a home.

"Most people wanted the younger boys and girls, six-and seven-year-olds. Helga was twelve and tall for her age. So she sat waiting in the assignment center until she was almost the last one remaining. That made her feel so...unwanted.

"Then this farm couple came in looking for an older child. They said Helga could live with them and they would send her to school if she would do some light chores in the farmhouse. So..."

I'm leaning forward, listening eagerly, when Mrs. F. stops short and flashes a quick smile at Helga and Mr. F., who have just entered the room. "How was your lunch?

Herman, bring a chair here for Helga. Tell me what you've been up to. Tell me about school."

I get up abruptly and give Helga the chair I've been using. What was Mrs. F. about to tell me? Now I'll never know. I still feel like the whole world—war and all—is resting on my shoulders.

Mr. F. passes around the box of chocolates that's been lying enticingly on the bedside table behind me all this time. I take one and excuse myself to go to the bathroom. Afterward, I wander up and down the hospital corridor a bit, peering nosily into some of the patients' rooms.

When I come back, the nurse has returned and tucked Mrs. F. back into bed. She looks tired, not nearly as fresh as when we first arrived. Some of her eyeliner is smudged and I wonder if she's been crying while talking to Helga, who has a blank expression and doesn't say much. But Mrs. F. urges us to stay just a little longer.

Mr. F. drives Helga and me home to the Bronx. My mother's invited him to stay and have dinner with us in honor of Arnold's being home on furlough. The moment I see my brother, I bury my head in the coarse khaki wool of his uniform jacket and I don't let go until he laughingly shakes me free.

If only we could stop the clock. Bring the world and all its mad, crazy, and evil carryings-on to a halt right here and now…even for a little while.

The table is set in the dining alcove with my mother's best china. The soup bowls are brimming. We all sit down and my father and Mr. F. raise their wine glasses across the table at each other. "To the health and safety of our boys and to VICTORY!"

"To PEACE and to the defeat of Hitler!" I add, raising my water glass so vigorously that it splashes a fountain of drops onto my mother's hand-embroidered linen tablecloth.

"Why, Isabel," my father remarks with an air of surprise, "I didn't know you could get so worked up about the war."

"So what do you think of my brother? He's pretty handsome in his uniform, isn't he?"

It's late, after our evening of celebration, and Helga and I are in my room getting ready for bed. Mr. F. has left to go back to his empty house in Westchester, and Arnold is sleeping in his usual place in the dining alcove.

"*Ja*," Helga agrees. "But better I think not in the uniform."

"Oh, of course, you're right. It would be wonderful if everything could go back to the way it was before the war…" I stop myself abruptly, remembering that Helga's memories of men and women and even children in uniforms goes back almost all her life to the time of the

Hitler Youth in the 1930s. *And when Jewish blood spurts from the knife…*

There is silence for a while, until Helga murmurs, "And so, good night."

But I'm much too occupied with thoughts of my interrupted conversation with Mrs. F. about the chicken farm, and it's impossible to close my eyes.

"Helga?"

*"Ja?"*

"Are you asleep yet? Could I talk to you for a minute?"

*"Ja?"*

"You know that paper I wrote for my history class about the *Kindertransport*?"

*"Ja?"*

"Well, my teacher Mrs. Boylan liked it very much. She wants me to write more about it. Like what happened next. You know, *after* the refugee children from Germany arrived in England."

This is all a terrible lie. In seventh-grade history we're studying the Middle Ages and Mrs. Boylan has never seemed to me to be the least bit interested in anything that has happened in Germany in the last few years. The so-called assignment that I wrote for her has been sitting in a box of letters, pictures, and souvenirs that I keep hidden under my bed.

"For example, where did you live when you first arrived in England? Your Aunt Harriette mentioned something to me about a…a chicken farm. I didn't even know they had chicken farms in England. Although that's silly, isn't it. Where else would they get eggs? And chicken?"

"Isabel, please," Helga interrupts my lame attempts to get her to describe her life as a twelve-year-old child separated from her family and in a strange, new setting. "I am worried so much about the health of Aunt Harriette. I cannot talk about this sad place that I was sent. I never want to talk about it."

I plop my head down onto my pillow in a mixture of disappointment and annoyance. "I don't mean to upset you, Helga. But, you know, if it was awful for you, you might feel a lot better if you talked about it."

There is no answer from the other bed. Now what am I supposed to do? What if I've only made things worse for Helga with all my nosy questions? But it really is more than just empty curiosity on my part. What *does* happen to somebody who is sent away from home and family, probably forever, and comes to a "sad place?"

What if it had happened to me? The very least I would want was for people to know about it. Helga's story, I believe, should be told.

"You know," I say as casually as I can to the continuing silence in the other bed, "if you don't want to talk about it, Helga, maybe you could *write* about it. Sometimes that's easier. And then we'd have a written report in your own words. How does that sound?"

I hold my breath in the dark. Is Helga asleep or just not speaking to me anymore?

"*Ach,*" a soft voice finally replies, "maybe someday I write it in German."

"German?" I'm up on my elbows and leaning over toward Helga's bed. "No! In English. And not 'someday.' Now. It doesn't matter how many mistakes you make. In fact, it will be good practice for school. Do you want to be stuck forever in seventh-grade English when you're supposed to be in ninth? Answer me, Helga."

"I think about it," Helga murmurs. "But there will be so many mistakes. Always, always there are too many mistakes."

# Thirteen

*Allons enfants de la patrie/Le jour de gloire est arrivé.*
We're learning the words to the *Marseillaise*, the national
anthem of France, in our intermediate French class.

Of course, as Miss Damore has already been forced
to admit and has explained to us, there is no indepen-
dent country known as France at the moment. The Nazis
invaded it in 1940, along with Holland and Belgium (as
well as Luxembourg, Denmark, and Norway).

The so-called Free French are hiding out in the
mountains of southern and eastern France, trying to hold
off advancing German control. They blow up trains and
munitions factories, and their snipers shoot the German
sentries that guard them. But things are looking pretty
grim nevertheless.

So, on behalf of the Free French, our class is chanting with military gusto, *Aux armes, citoyens! Formez vos
bataillons. Marchons, marchons, qu'un sang impur.* Miss
Damore has decided that we're going to learn as many
verses as we can, and then translate them into English.

Without even raising his hand, Billy Crosby blurts

out—like the show-off that he is—that France will be free before we even finish translating the *Marseillaise*. Because, he says boastfully, "the U.S. and the Brits are going to invade it any day now."

"*En français*, Billy," Miss Damore cautions him in her charming accent.

I glance across the aisle at Mr. Smiley-Face. Aside from the fact that Billy is dead wrong (we're still struggling to push the Germans out of North Africa so we can invade southern Europe sometime next year), he is hardly up to saying all this in French, a rule that Miss Damore made the first day of the term. I console myself with the fact that even if we *don't* get to the subjunctive, maybe Billy will flunk out of the class just for being a wise guy.

It's agony sitting across the aisle from him twice a week. He's forever leaving stupid offerings on my desk… sticky peppermint candies and pencils with no erasers that are decorated with colored feathers. He draws dumb pictures of the other kids in the class and passes them to me with little "guess who" hints.

How do I know he isn't sending drawings of me around the room to other people…elongating my nose and exaggerating my breasts, which he never seems to stop looking at. If he just wants to annoy me, that's one thing. But if he actually *likes* me, then I've got to find a way to get rid of him. Why is it so hard to tell?

Billy is now struggling with the French words for *before*, *finish*, *translate*, *free*, *invade*, and the verb forms he needs to repeat his misinformation in French. With my eyes fixed on the wooden grooves and inky smears on my desk, I'm actually enjoying listening to him struggle with something as easy as "Before we finish…" *(Avant de finir…)*.

In fact, fool that I am, I'm quietly mouthing the words to myself when Miss Damore calls my name and asks me to help Billy get his sentence started. *"Pouvez-vous, Mademoiselle Isabel, aider votre ami?"*

*"Ami"*…my boyfriend? Hardly! I turn to Billy almost crossly and supply him with the French words, in response to which his eyes sparkle and his mouth grows more smiley than ever. Only the chiming of the bell announcing the end of the period saves me from further embarrassment. Grabbing my books, I flee into the corridor and gallop down the staircase.

"Hey, Frenchy."

It's the end of the last period of the day and I'm heading back to homeroom. I hardly need to turn around. It's Billy again, his glasses glinting and a self-assured smile wreathing his face. "What did ya run away for? I wanted to thank you for savin' me from Damore, at least until the bell rung. Boy, she's got a nerve askin' for a translation of a long sentence like that."

I shift my books to my other arm and sigh. "Well,

you should have known better than to call out. Anyhow, what you said was wrong. Nobody on our side of the war is ready to invade France yet. A landing anywhere on the French coast is still a long way off."

"Oh yeah? Shows how much you know. I got secret information. My Pop's on the inside."

Billy makes me so mad I could spit. "Why? Because he's a police detective?"

"*And* a Civil Defense air raid warden *and* on the bomb squad. You'll be glad some day when he and his team save the whole neighborhood from an enemy attack. He's also a blackout warden. So be sure to follow the rules for the next blackout." Billy looks at me teasingly. "I know where you live, Frenchy."

I turn into the door of homeroom with Billy following, wondering how I could possibly be unlucky enough to attract such a person.

"Hey," Billy grabs my arm, "how about comin' to the movies with me on Saturday? You know, to thank you for helping me out in French."

Speechless, I plop down at my desk. This is really too much. I've never in my life gone on a "date" to the movies with a boy. Even if I wanted to—and I certainly don't with Billy—my mother wouldn't let me.

"Yeah, come on," says Billy, as Mr. Jeffers indicates for him to take his seat. "It'll be fun…*The Commandos Strike at Dawn*…you ain't seen it yet, did ya?"

"What was that all about?" Sibby wants to know as we start walking home together. Helga is staying after school today for some tutoring in English grammar.

When I tell her, she starts to chant, "Boyfriend, boyfriend, Izzie's got a boyfriend."

"Don't you dare, Sybil Simon," I exclaim. "I'm only telling you this because you saw him talking to me in class. I wouldn't even admit it otherwise. Billy Crosby is anything but my type. He's goofy-looking, and he's stuck-up and dumb all at the same time. He's fresh, too. He never takes his eyes off my chest. Can you just imagine how he'd act in a dark movie theater?"

Sibby giggles. "So who is your type? What do you think about...*Bing Crosby*? You don't suppose he might be a relative of Billy?"

"No, I don't. And to tell you the truth, Bing Crosby might be a good crooner but I don't think much of his looks either. His face reminds me of a glass of warm milk."

"Boy, are you picky, Izzie. Oh, I know who you would really go for, especially if you were looking for 'cute'... Frank Sinatra. My mom and I heard him on the radio last night singing 'I'll Never Smile Again.' Leona said if she ever saw him in person, she'd probably pass out."

"You think? He's awfully skinny from the pictures I've seen of him. More likely, he'd be the one to pass out."

"You're so sarcastic, Izzie. I sort of agree with you about Bing Crosby. He's losing his hair and he's got an awful lot of kids. But Sinatra, wow… If he ever gets to be in the stage show at some big Broadway movie theater, my mom and I want to go. If my mom can't take time off from work, will you go with me? Say yes."

"Yes," I say wearily. "If it's okay with my mother. And we'll have to take Helga, too. Except she really makes me nervous these days. Did you notice how jumpy she is lately? She always seems to be looking behind her. Instead of relaxing now that she's out of Germany and out of England, she acts like she's getting more suspicious of people all the time."

"Well, you would be, too, if you had been separated from your family, thrown together with a lot of strange kids, and sent to a foreign country where people weren't too welcoming. Then she came here and got put down at school, insulted at the USO, and picked up by the police. By the way, did she ever write that description for you of what happened to her after she got to England?"

"Not yet, although she seems to be doing a lot of scribbling lately. Maybe it's just her extra homework. I can't keep asking her. She looks like she's ready to cry most of the time."

Arnold's two-day furlough went by so fast, it might just as well have been two hours. This time he had a travel pass from the Army and he took the train down to Grand Central Station and then the railroad to some place in Massachusetts. It doesn't seem like he's going directly to flight-training school after all. But who can ever tell with the Army?

He had to leave the apartment at five-thirty in the morning, so our farewells were sleepy and confused and maybe that was all to the good. What do you say to someone you love and who you might not see again for a very long time, or maybe even…?

We now have a blue star on the door of our apartment. Some people put them in the windows of their houses, but who's going to look up at the fourth floor of an apartment building to make out a blue star in the window?

Let's just hope the star remains a blue one—it shows that a son or brother or husband is serving in the war. A gold star—and some have already begun to appear— means that someone who was serving has been killed.

Mealtimes have been a downbeat affair ever since Arnold left. Tonight, my mother and father start arguing again about what plans the Army has for Arnold. "I'll be just as happy," my mother remarks, "if they forget all about putting my son into the cockpit of some flimsy airplane. He might be a lot safer on the ground."

"That's the silliest thing I ever heard," my father retorts, as my mother's baked salmon loaf and mashed potatoes get passed around the table to Helga and me. "Don't you know that the infantry is the most dangerous of all the divisions. It's always the foot soldiers who get the worst of it in a war."

"I didn't *say* I wanted to see him in the infantry." My mother shrugs and tosses her head with an air of annoyance. "There are lots of other important and useful jobs in the Army that don't involve crashing an airplane or being shot at in the mud."

I can't imagine what Helga is making of this conversation between my parents. It must sound so stupid to her after all she's seen and been through, especially in Germany where her own father has been imprisoned by the Nazis in a labor camp.

We're just finishing our meal with a dessert of baked apples when the screeching wail of the air-raid siren down on the street beneath our windows goes off. This is the first blackout we've had since Helga came to live with us (they started last spring) and I can't help wondering if it could possibly have anything to do with Billy Crosby's warning of this afternoon. *I know where you live, Frenchy.* Ugh!

The radio stays on but the blackout curtains are drawn and most of the lights will have to be put out, just in case it's a real attack. Fortunately it never has been (German bombers have made it to England but not to the Bronx).

Helga, however, immediately goes running off to the

bedroom that we share and comes back with her coat, her school briefcase, and a sheaf of papers. "Here, Isabel, this is for you," she says, shoving the loose pages at me. "You can read them in the cellar where we go now. It will perhaps be a long time. Where is your coat?"

I'm completely confused. My parents have already made themselves comfortable in the living room beside the radio. I reach for Helga's hand in the semi-darkness. "No, no, we don't need our coats. We're not going anywhere."

Helga shakes her head stubbornly. "Isabel, it is not safe to stay here. Always in England we go to the root cellar on the farm, or into the basement of the youth hostel. Perhaps that is the best place." She glances toward the living room. "You must explain this to your parents. Here, so far above the ground, it is most dangerous to remain."

Since I can't seem to convince Helga that this is just an air-raid drill and not a real alert that enemy airplanes are on their way, I ask my father to explain it to her.

"No, no, no, my dear," he tells her with his usual air of authority. "The Germans haven't got bombers that are long-range enough to hit the Eastern U.S. And neither have the Japs. So nothing to worry about. Just sit back and relax until the all-clear siren sounds."

But Helga still has questions. She retreats to the bedroom, murmuring, "If there is no possible danger of attack, what do we practice for? This I cannot believe."

I'm still holding the loose pages that Helga gave me. Can these possibly be the written account I've been waiting for of her first experience of England? I rattle the pages at her. "This is for me to read?"

"*Ja*. But now we must remain in the dark. So you cannot." And she reaches out to take them back from me.

"No." I hold onto them tightly. "I'll keep them till the lights come on. Or…" I hop onto my bed, "I'll read them by flashlight under the covers."

Helga's voice is choked and low. "I am ashamed to write and complain about these things that have happened. Others have suffered more and surely died because of me. You must promise me, Isabel that, after you read what I have written, you will not ask me any questions and we will never talk about this again." Her figure looms over me in the dark.

I clutch Helga's confession to my chest. "Why are you ashamed? It's Hitler and his Nazi murderers who should be ashamed."

"No, Isabel, you don't understand. That is not the way it works."

I shake my head in bafflement, grab my flashlight, and dive under the covers to start reading the story of Helga's life as a Kindertransport child on an English chicken farm, far from her home and family.

# Fourteen

*Isabel,*

*I already told you about the* Kindertransport *train to the port in Holland and then the ferry to Harwich. Mutti said that soon our entire family would come together again in England. I knew this could never come true. What about Papa? Since the autumn of 1939, he was a prisoner in the Buchenwald camp in Germany, working in the stone quarry with his bare hands to build roads for the Nazi commanders. So much we knew.*

*We Kinder arrived at last to the assignment center. Some children already had sponsors who came to take them to their homes. Other people came to look at us with judging eyes. Were we clean, healthy, obedient-looking…and young? Even babies were chosen. But those of us who were taller like me, or older, were not.*

*By darkness, we were six or more left, mostly boys. The officials in charge of the refugee children said they would take us to an orphanage. A man and woman came in as we were putting our things into an Army truck to be transported. She was tall, with thin lips and black hair pulled into a tight* knot. He was stout and gray-bearded with tiny watery eyes.

"How old is this one?" they asked. I told them I am twelve. "You look older," they said. "Have you finished with school?"

"No," I told them, in German. "I want to go to school so I can learn English."

The refugee officer translated for them and they went away to talk between themselves. Then they returned.

"We'll take her," they said. "She can help out on the farm and go to school in the village."

"Do you agree?" the officer asked. I said yes. I did not want to go to the orphanage. My things were taken off the Army transport and I went into the farm truck with the Rathbones. That was their name.

The farmhouse was old and dark, with stone floors and small windows. My room was under the eaves. I went up the ladder with candlelight and I was very homesick and unhappy. All that first night I wept. Better to be with Papa in Buchenwald, or hiding in a coal bin with Mama's relatives.

The next day I learned my duties. I must feed the chickens before walking three miles to the village school. After school I must sweep and dust and scrub the floors. Also, I must look after Tim. Tim is their son. He is born with a defect. He has slanting eyes like a Mongolian and a broad face. His body is short, thick, and heavy. He is ten years old.

Tim is not bad or wicked and he likes to hug and wrestle, not knowing his own strength. Yet he must be tended all the *time. Slime and drool must be wiped from his nose and lips. Often he soils himself. Soon he follows me everywhere, even when I walk to school, sometimes even to my room where I try to do my homework.*

*There is also the problem of the school...*

Helga's writing trails off and I hurl myself out from under the covers. My flashlight has begun to dim and, with that, the all-clear siren goes off. The blackout is over. Lights flash on everywhere, in the apartment and the street below.

"Helga!" I exclaim, "I can't believe you lived like that for such a long time. And what happened at the school? You didn't finish writing your story."

All this time Helga must have been lying quietly on her bed. "It is too much to tell, Isabel," she says softly. "And looking up every word for correct spelling, I got so tired. Let us now forget all about it."

"No, we can't. You must tell me the rest if the writing is too hard. The school that was three miles away in the village...what about it?"

Helga is sitting on the edge of her bed and I on mine. Our knees are almost touching. To my relief she starts to talk.

"The village is small and the school is only for the early grades. Because I speak such poor English I am put in the lowest grade with the youngest children. This makes me feel very stupid. But the schoolmaster says I must start at the beginning because I have to be taught not to think in German. And also because I am late many days.

"Some days I cannot come at all. The Rathbones have so many chores for me to do. More than feeding and watering the birds, they want me to clean out the waste from the chicken coops.

"They never smile. We eat our meals in silence. The only people who come to the farm are the sellers of eggs and chickens who buy what they raise. For company I have only Tim who stays close to me more and more. So I cannot drive him away."

I don't want to stop Helga but I can't keep myself from interrupting. "They sound like terrible people. They're not even kind and loving to their little boy."

Helga shakes her head. "They are not really cruel. Just silent and disappointed, I think, that their child is defective. I am a refugee in England—no other country will take us—and it is not my place to speak against them."

I think about this. True, the Rathbones rescued Helga from a terrible fate if she had remained in Germany between 1939 and 1942, when her uncle was able to bring her to America. As Leona Simon has told me, only a small number of Jewish children were admitted to the U.S. at that time, as compared with 10,000 Jewish and non-Jewish Kindertransport children taken in by England.

"One day," Helga continues, "when Tim follows me to school, the children who live near the village begin to throw pebbles at us. This has happened before and they are only small pebbles. Tim laughs and tries to throw some back. He is, after all, looking for playmates.

"This time, though, the pebbles become stones. I try to shelter us and start to run back to the farm with Tim. The children are of all ages. They are shouting at us, *The idiot and the Jew, get off with you! No one wants you here. Get off with you.*

"Tim is clumsy and also he doesn't want to run away. First I pull him and then I try to push him from behind. But he thinks this is fun. Now the children are throwing larger and heavier stones and they are chasing us. Some of the stones are hitting our shoulders and the backs of our legs. Tim is starting to become frightened. He runs and trips and nearly falls.

"I try to hold him up. This slows us down. It is too late to escape our attackers. One of the older and bigger boys heaves a heavy rock. It strikes Tim in the head and he falls to the ground. There is blood everywhere."

"They really said that…*the idiot and the Jew*! I would have punched them in the mouth, every single one of them, even the littlest kids. It's never too early to learn a lesson about not calling people names. Oh gosh, Helga, I wish I was there…me and Sibby and…and Leona. We'd have smacked them around but good."

The door to our room opens abruptly and my mother is standing there with an exasperated expression. "What is all this shrieking about, Isabel? Your father would like to know. He can hardly hear the radio."

Suddenly I'm back in our apartment in the Bronx, a long way from the narrow country road somewhere in England where Helga and Tim were stoned by the local children. "It's…it's nothing. Just something that Helga was telling me about the…the Kindertransport. You remember?"

My mother looks at Helga, who is pale and quiet. "Well, I hoped you two weren't fighting. Did the black-out upset you, Helga?"

Helga shakes her head. *"Ach, nein."*

I can't wait for my mother to leave so I can hear the rest. Finally she does.

"What happened to Tim?" I gasp in a loud whisper.

"I got him back to the farm. His head wound healed, but he became more sick in many other ways. His parents blamed me for what happened to him and I took care of him from then on all of the time, working also on the farm. I never went back to the school. About a year later, Tim died. After that, I went to live in the hostel near the Army camp. I told you before that it was right that I should be punished when I arrived to England. And that is what happened."

"But why, Helga? What did you do that was so

horrible? Why should you have been punished?"

"No more questions, Isabel. You promised."

"Creamed onions and cauliflower *au gratin*," Sibby informs me. "My mom says to tell your mother that's what we're bringing. And thanks a lot for inviting us to dinner."

The month of November has slipped by and everybody is getting ready for the first wartime Thanksgiving. The whole country is in a tizzy about the holiday this year. Because of rationing, it's hard to get butter for mashed potatoes or sugar for pies and desserts. Even turkeys and chickens are a little on the scarce side.

And, on top of that, President Roosevelt recently announced that coffee is going to be rationed. Starting on November 29, three days after Thanksgiving, Americans will be limited to one cup of coffee per day. It isn't because of a coffee shortage. There's plenty of coffee in Brazil. And also there's plenty of sugar in Cuba. It's because of the scarcity of ships—which are needed to carry soldiers and weapons abroad—that are available to bring these luxuries to American tables.

Sibby and I don't drink coffee, so we couldn't care less. I do think, though, that my mother isn't going to be too thrilled with Leona Simon's contribution of creamed onions and cauliflower *au gratin*. We usually have candied sweet potatoes and buttered green peas for vegetables on Thanksgiving.

"What, by the way, is cauliflower *au gratin*?" I ask Sybil.

"You don't know?" she clucks. "It's French. Guess you'll have to ask your boyfriend, Billy."

I hate it when Sibby teases me about Billy Crosby, whom I sincerely detest. "Never mind. I'll look it up."

"Oh, don't bother. It's just breadcrumbs and cheese sprinkled on top of the cauliflower. You know Leona. She's always trying to make vegetables taste better. She says we all have to plant Victory Gardens next spring because meat rationing is going to get even stricter." Sibby sniffs. "Can't you just see us trying to grow dinner in a window box here in the Bronx?"

I really must dash off a letter to Ruthie before the holiday weekend. I know that Helga doesn't want me to tell anybody about her hardworking life on the chicken farm, about the weirdly silent Rathbones who wouldn't let her go to school, and about poor slobbering but loving Tim who died when he was only eleven. But I owe it to Ruthie to answer her questions, especially the ones about Helga.

*Dear Ruthie,*

*How are you? No, of course, I'm not mad at you. Are you at me? I have so much to tell you. But I waited to be able to give you the whole story about Helga and the chicken farm, which I found out happened in*

*England, not in Germany.*

*I'm going to write Helga's story in the form of a composition—or I guess you could call it a biography—on a separate piece of paper attached to this letter. It starts with when she left her family in Germany and went to England with a bunch of other Jewish refugee children on something called a Kindertransport. You'll understand everything when you read it.*

*Now for a surprise. "Do I ever see or hear from Helga?" She's been living with us here in the apartment since school began! She also goes to my junior high, where she has mostly ninth-grade classes but not all. Her Aunt Harriette, Mrs. Frankfurter (I call her Mrs. F.) took sick after they got back from Shady Pines and had a serious operation.*

*We're better friends now than we were up at the hotel, but Helga is still hard to know really well. She says mysterious things about telling lies and having to be punished for them. I don't understand.*

*Arnold joined the Air Force and he came home on furlough for two days when he was transferred from New Jersey to Massachusetts. He looks so handsome in his uniform. Helga had a letter from Roy telling her he was on a ship in the Pacific. That's all I know on the romance side.*

*This will be Helga's first Thanksgiving. We're having company—my friend Sybil and her mother from the building and Helga's aunt and uncle now that she's feeling better. Have a Happy Thanksgiving.*

*Love, Izzie*

*P.S. A boy in my French class likes me. He stares at my chest all the time and asked me to go to the movies with him. It's a war movie, of course…* The Commandos Strike at Dawn. *I actually hate him. What do you think I should do?*

# Fifteen

"To our absent loved ones," my father declares, raising his wineglass in a toast as we all sit down to Thanksgiving dinner in the crowded dining space in our apartment. Everybody joins in, including Sibby and me who, instead of wine, are drinking ginger ale with maraschino cherries, otherwise known as Shirley Temples.

Each of us, of course, has special absent loved ones in mind. My parents and I are thinking of Arnold, who now writes that he might soon be shipped overseas. This makes no sense to us because he hasn't had his Air Force training yet and what if they send him to North Africa before he even learns to fly a plane?

Sybil and Leona are surely thinking of Mr. Simon somewhere in the submarine-infested waters of the stormy North Atlantic, trying to steer a ship loaded with war supplies to a safe harbor in England.

And Helga, what is she thinking about? There's Roy, of course, somewhere in the Pacific, where the war against the Japanese still isn't going well. But she has more absent loved ones than any of us…her father, last known to have been in the German prison camp of Buchenwald, and her mother and two sisters hiding out in fearfully dangerous German-occupied Holland.

I would have thought that Helga's non-Jewish *Mutti* would have been able to save herself and her daughters. "But marriage to a Jew, or having one Jewish parent," Helga has told me, "is a black mark. In the case of a child, of course, Jewish blood runs in the veins." And I'm reminded again, at our festive and abundant Thanksgiving table, of the Hitler Youth song, *And when Jewish blood spurts from the knife…*

But in spite of everything, I try to think of today as a cheery occasion. For one thing, it's the start of a four-day school holiday. Already, Mrs. F. has invited Helga and me to visit her in Westchester this weekend. "And Sybil must come, too," she adds. "You girls can have a lovely time. There's skating, horseback riding, hiking in the woods."

Mr. F. places his hand on Mrs. F.'s ring-studded fingers in a cautioning gesture.

"Oh," she laughs, "Herman thinks I'm not well enough yet. Of course, I wouldn't be able to do any outdoor sports with you girls. But we'd still have fun. And the housekeeper is there to take care of meals and laundry." Her black-rimmed eyes look around the room anxiously.

As soon as Mrs. F. came in the door, I couldn't help

noticing how much thinner she looked than before her operation. It had been hard to tell how much weight she'd lost when I saw her in the hospital, wrapped in her bedazzling dressing gowns and cuddly blankets.

Today, though, her normally full cheeks look sunken and her chin seems to have become rather pointed beneath her—as usual—expertly applied makeup. She is beautifully dressed, however, in a honey-toned mink coat and matching hat, worn over a dressy suit of amber-colored velvet studded with a gleaming gold brooch.

"You never told me how glamorous she was," Sibby whispered after she'd been introduced. "She could be a movie star, one of the older really dramatic ones who scratch out the eyes of the men who've wronged them."

Now, as my father carves the turkey and my mother passes the laden plates around the table, Mr. F. and Leona Simon find themselves talking about the special Day of Mourning and Prayer that is to take place in New York City just about a week from now. Its purpose is to call attention to the Jews who are trapped in Nazi-dominated Europe and have no hope of being able to escape to any other country. Synagogues, radio stations, and stores and factories will have special services.

Mr. F. thinks this is a good way to awaken Americans to the fact that Jews all over Europe are being rounded up and thrown into labor camps. But Leona thinks it's too late to do much good. "If you read the teeny, tiny little reports that are tucked away in the corners of the newspapers," she tells Mr. F., "you'll learn that the Germans have built at least half a dozen new camps this year in Poland alone."

Leona pauses and glances around the table, noticing that Helga and Mrs. F. are busily involved in some sort of private conversation. "And," she adds confidentially to her listeners, who now include my parents as well as Sibby and me, "they don't call them labor camps anymore. Or prison camps. They call them concentration camps."

"What," I pipe up, "are they concentrating on?"

"Oh, sweetie," Leona replies, in a completely different tone of voice. "Here come our plates of delicious food. Do you and Sybil need refills of your Shirley Temples?"

Without waiting for an answer, she snatches our glasses off the table and disappears into the kitchen.

Why didn't Leona answer my question? I jump up and follow her. I have a hunch she was about to say something important and dreadful that would be very upsetting, and that she didn't want certain people at the table to hear...especially Helga.

Leona is busily pouring ginger ale and adding bright red cherry juice and extra cherries to our glasses.

"You didn't answer me in there, about the...the concentration camps."

"Isabel, you shouldn't be in here. This isn't a good time to talk. The concentration camps are connected with something the Nazis are doing now to the Jews in Germany. It's called the 'Final Solution'."

"The Final...Solution?" I'm getting the idea that this has nothing to do with the algebra problems that have been giving me big headaches in Mrs. Deutsch's math class.

Leona gives me a shove and I return to my seat at the table. My mother raises her eyebrows questioningly, but happily she doesn't comment on my brief absence. I'm not known for rushing into the kitchen to try to be helpful during meals.

I dig into my plate of turkey, stuffing, sweet potatoes, cranberry sauce, and Leona Simon's creamed onions and cauliflower *au gratin*. Something seems to have taken the edge off my appetite. I poke away even at the good stuff. The creamed onions, of course, are terrible, the cauliflower not quite so bad, probably because of the French *au gratin* touch.

Sibby takes a look at my face. Then she pokes my arm. "Hide the onions under a turkey slice," she advises. "You're not going to throw up, are you, Izzie?"

"Shut up," I whisper. "I'm not. And don't try to give me ideas."

Everybody else at the table seems to be having a wonderful time, talking and eating and drinking. My father and Mr. F. are having a lively discussion about the American and British landings in German-controlled

North Africa earlier this month, and they are predicting an invasion of Italy sometime next year. Mrs. F. is getting a little bit tipsy during a gossipy exchange with my mother. Leona is talking to me, Sibby, and Helga about Frank Sinatra maybe doing a holiday show at the Paramount. Even Helga looks happy.

The meal ends with Mr. F. popping the cork on a bottle of champagne that he and Mrs. F. have brought to the party, along with a lavish assortment of holiday pies and desserts. "I think all the girls should have a sip as well," Mrs. F. announces. "One day this terrible war will end in victory and our darlings will all grow up and have 'champagne' lives!"

Champagne—the very name of this pale bubbly wine sounds so exciting. Skillfully, Mr. F. fills eight thin-stemmed crystal glasses and places one before each of us. Since we've already toasted our absent loved ones, my parents suggest we drink to Harriette Frankfurter's continuing recovery and wish her a return to perfect health.

Mrs. F. objects and begins to dab at her eyes with a lacy handkerchief. "Oh, no, not me," she protests. "I'm well already. To all those everywhere who are suffering so much as a result of this war."

But we've already raised our glasses and are toasting the health of Mrs. F., whose eyeliner has begun to run in rivulets down her cheeks. I put my glass to my lips. The rim of it is so thin that it feels like, if I squeezed it too hard, it would shatter into a thousand tiny crystal shards. So this is champagne.

I take a swallow, exploding bubbles go shooting up my nose, and my mouth is instantly filled with the stinging, acid flavor that comes from biting (once on a dare) into a dead June bug.

"Isabel!" my mother exclaims. "Where are your manners? Leave the table at once!"

My soaking napkin and I arrive in the kitchen, where I'm frantically rinsing my mouth with water when Sybil appears at my side. "Honest to goodness, Izzie, you're so unsophisticated. Didn't you know that champagne tastes like sour ginger ale?"

"No," I say, between gulps of water. "You could have warned me. And anyhow that's a lie. It tastes *much* worse."

Poor Mrs. F.—by the time she and Mr. F. leave, she looks haggard from crying her happy tears and drinking too many toasts in wine and champagne.

"Having the girls visit you this weekend, Harriette, is out of the question," my mother states firmly, as Mrs. F. is being helped into her mink. "You're exhausted just from the effort of being out for the day instead of getting your usual amount of rest."

Mrs. F., whose mink hat is sitting tilted a little too far

to one side on her curled coppery hair, protests that she is "fine, just fine." But Mr. F., standing directly behind her, shakes his head to indicate that he agrees with my mother.

Then a last-minute decision is made. Helga will throw some clothes together and go home with the Frankfurters. It is, after all, her "real" home, and she can stay with her aunt and uncle until school opens on Monday.

"No need to take anything but a toothbrush, dear," Mrs. F. calls out, as I follow Helga into our bedroom to help her pack. "We'll buy you an entire winter wardrobe on the weekend."

"Sounds like you're going to have fun," I say, as I watch Helga gathering pajamas and underwear to take along. "You really want to go, don't you?"

"*Ja*. It is good that I go. But she is very sick. You see that, don't you?"

"Um, well your aunt does look a lot thinner than before the operation. But that's normal I guess…"

My mother is at the door to hurry Helga up because Mrs. F. is waiting in her coat and Mr. F. has already gone to get the car. We walk Helga and her aunt to the elevator and wave goodbye. It would have been fun for Sibby and me to go up to Westchester with Helga for skating and horseback riding. But I guess it's not to be.

As the elevator door is about to close, I get a last

look at Mrs. F. and Helga. Mrs. F. is leaning against the railing for support and suddenly appears to be in pain. Helga stands beside her, tall and willowy, suitcase in hand, her expression empty and forlorn.

It's the Saturday afternoon of the Thanksgiving weekend and Sibby and I are at loose ends. After having had a disagreement about which movie to go to, it looks like we're not going to either. Sybil wants to go down to Times Square to see a romantic new spy thriller with Humphrey Bogart called *Casablanca*. I'm not sure we'll be able to get in because it's a first-run showing and Times Square is just overflowing with soldiers and sailors and everybody else who's having a holiday fling.

"So I suppose you just want to hang out in this boring neighborhood near home and see Judy Garland in *For Me and My Gal*. Or would you prefer something really juvenile like *Bambi*, the story of the adorable little baby deer?"

"You don't have to get nasty about it," I tell Sybil. "Anyhow, what's wrong with Judy Garland?"

"She's too sweet and sappy. And those big cow eyes."

"But she can sing, you have to admit that."

I make one last suggestion. "How about we just go shopping?"

"With what? I don't have any money."

"Window shopping. You know."

Immediately behind me, I hear a high-pitched voice mimicking my own. *Window shopping, you know.* Somebody taps me hard on the shoulder. I turn around and find myself face to face with Billy Crosby.

"Uh-oh," Sibby remarks. If she says the word *boyfriend*, I'll kill her right here in front of the movie theater, where Judy Garland is grinning at us from a huge color poster.

Billy's lips are curled into one of his exasperating smiles. "Girls! Nothing on your minds but shopping. There's a bunch of stuff you could be doing for the war effort."

"Who asked you?" I demand.

Billy holds his ground. "Want a list?"

"No thanks," I answer freshly. "We already rolled bandages, collected scrap metal, made tinfoil and rubber-band balls, bought defense stamps, and served sandwiches at the USO. I even tried knitting a scarf for *if* and *when* we invade France. What else am I supposed to do?" I poke Sybil. "Oh, and her mother is working at a defense job. In a shipyard."

"Gosh, Frenchy," Billy says, hunching his soldiers, his glasses glinting, "you don't have to be so mad about everything. What's eatin' you, anyway?"

"You are. You act like you always know everything, like you're ten miles ahead of everybody else. What makes you such a show-off?"

Sybil is shifting her weight from one foot to the other, hands on her hips, and staring down at the sidewalk.

"Honest," Billy is suddenly pleading. "I'm not. I just thought if you wanted to get behind the war effort. But now I sorta see…"

"Listen," Sibby suddenly explodes at the two of us. "If the both of you are just going to stand around here arguing, I'm going downtown to see the movie I wanted to see in the first place." And, without another word, she turns and runs off toward the subway station entrance at the end of the block.

Before I can make a quick dash after her, Sibby is lost in the crowd. I stand there looking blankly in her direction.

"Aw, let her go," Billy advises. "She's even more hot-tempered than you are, Frenchy. Anyhow, I got a suggestion." Billy clears his throat. *"Voulez-vous faire une petite promenade avec moi?"*

What am I going to do now? Sybil has done one of the worst things a friend can do. She's run out on me and I'm stuck with Billy, who wants me to take a little walk with him.

Hmm…*une petite promenade.* Amazingly, Billy got the sentence right. And his accent wasn't bad either.

Why, I wonder, does everything sound so much better in French?

# Sixteen

"So what's the story with the German girl?" Billy wants to know.

We're walking around and around the park, the one with the slimy fountain pond into which Sibby and I dipped our feet on that hot day when I'd just gotten home from Shady Pines, and where I told Sybil about Helga—and Roy.

Today, though, there's a November chill in the air and a gusty wind. And the way I see Helga is a whole lot different from the way I did then. I was so stupidly envious of her during our time together at Moskin's. Everyone crowded around her with questions and compliments. Harry the waiter and the busboys treated her like a princess. And then Roy came along and rescued her from a vicious farm dog—and became her prince.

"You mean Helga?"

"Yeah. Frankfurter."

"I think that's disgustingly mean. Those kids at school calling her Helga Hot Dog. I just hope, Billy Crosby, that you're not one of them."

Billy's right hand shoots up. "I swear I never called her that. You're always pickin' on me, Frenchy. What'd I ever do?"

"*Frankfurter* just means her family once came from Frankfurt in Germany. Hot dogs do, too. But it's still insulting. Also, she had to get away from Germany. Nowadays, they'd kill her over there in a minute. Because she's half Jewish."

Billy nods. "So then she can't be a spy, I guess."

"Did anybody ever really think she was? Did you? A fourteen-year-old girl, a spy? How dumb is that?"

Billy has started throwing pebbles into the pond. "Not impossible," he replies nonchalantly. "Don't you read those girlie books like Nancy Drew or whoever?"

I pick up a handful of pebbles and start throwing them at the fountain, too. The target in my imagination, though, is Billy. "Nancy Drew isn't a spy," I tell him sharply. "She's a detective."

"Okay, okay," he says, "calm down, Frenchy."

It's pretty clear that Billy Crosby and I will never get along. The minute he turns smart-alecky I start getting mad at him. I get more and more furious until he sort of gives in without actually apologizing. I go along with that for a while until he starts to annoy me all over again. If that's what goes on between men and women all through life, this might be a very good time to quit trying to be friends with a boy.

I pull my knee-length winter coat tighter around me. I'm wearing penny loafers and socks, no stockings. "Listen, Billy, I'm cold. I'm going home."

Billy drops his handful of pebbles. "Aw, gee, Frenchy, don't go. See, I knew we shoulda gone to the movies this afternoon."

"Oh, really? Guess I didn't hear you. Or didn't you know how to say that in French?"

Ignoring my sarcasm, Billy has actually hung an arm around my shoulders and started to propel me out of the park. It seems like he's going to walk me home, even though it's not in the same direction as where he lives. But the next thing I know he's steering me through the entrance of Hansen's Drugstore and, a moment later, we're both perched on tall wooden stools at the marble soda fountain.

It always smells wonderful in Hansen's. Chocolate syrup, malted milks, ice cream sodas and sundaes, even the delicious odor of toasted bacon sandwiches, mingle with the faint scent of pharmaceuticals that comes from the prescription department all the way in the back. It's nice and warm in here, too.

Billy orders a cherry Coke, so I do, too. I could really go for a banana split or a hot chocolate with whipped cream. But what if he's going to pay and he doesn't have enough money? On the other hand, why should he pay for me? Because it was his idea? What if it was Sibby and me? No matter whose idea it was, we'd each pay for ourselves.

This is all so confusing.

Anyhow, we sip our cherry Cokes without any more arguing, Billy pays, and I say, *Merci beaucoup*, to which Billy answers, *Il n'y a pas de quoi*. As dictated by Miss Damore, this is the correct response, meaning *don't mention it*.

Then we're outside in front of Hansen's in the early November dusk. Billy's eyeglasses catch the fading light and he flashes me a smile that seems more like a warning. "See ya in homeroom on Monday, Frenchy."

I can't think of another thing to say. Suddenly I'm terribly embarrassed at having spent an afternoon with Billy and gone to a soda fountain with him. Was this a date? Does his having bought me a cherry Coke mean that I am bound to him in some way?

Am I no longer free to be me?

I nod and waggle the fingers of my right hand at Billy. Then I feel like an idiot. Without a word, I turn and march off down the street toward home.

Even though I haven't been walking that fast, my heart is still pounding as I step into the lobby of our apartment building. My afternoon with Billy has left me feeling perplexed and jittery. He's only a twelve-year-old kid like me (although he made a point of letting me know that he was a lot closer to thirteen than I am), so why did I get such an odd creepy feeling when he slung his arm around me? Did his arm around my neck mean that he liked me or that he was the boss? Was the feeling nice or was it icky? Why can't I just shake off this last encounter with Billy the way I have all the others?

On top of that, I'm really upset with Sybil for the way she walked out on me right there in front of Judy Garland. I can't believe that Sibby actually got on the train and went to Times Square to see *Casablanca*. It just isn't the kind of thing she'd do without me. Probably she's home by now and this would be a good time to straighten out whatever it was that happened between us.

But when I ring the bell at the door of Sibby's apartment, it's Leona who answers. She's in her housecoat, smoking a cigarette, and listening to soft music on the radio.

"Oh, it's you, Isabel. I thought you and Sybil were spending the afternoon together. Did you kids have a fight?"

Suddenly I realize what a terrible mess I've gotten myself into by stopping off here. If Sibby really did go downtown all by herself and wasn't supposed to, I certainly don't want to tell on her. On the other hand, almost anything else I say will be a lie.

"We…um…got separated."

Leona takes a puff on her cigarette and looks doubtful. "Whatever that means. Sit down anyway. I'm sure she'll be home soon."

I flop down into one of Leona's sagging but really comfortable chairs. "You know," I say in the most normal fashion I can muster, "you and I never did finish our conversation on Thanksgiving. You were telling me about the concentration camps in Germany. You were going to explain…"

"Poland," Leona corrects me. "There are plenty of camps in Germany, of course, like the one they sent Helga's father to. But the newer camps are in Poland. The Nazis are using them to carry out the 'Final Solution.' I told you about that the other day…"

I pull myself forward and am sitting on the edge of my seat in Leona's shabby armchair. "The 'Final Solution'— it's not the same thing as solving a math problem, is it?"

"Well, yes. In a way it is. Question—what should we do to get rid of six million Jews from all over Europe? Answer—herd them together in concentration camps, put them to death with poison gas, and burn their bodies in the camp's cremation ovens. The smoke from the ovens goes up the chimneys and is carried away by the wind… poof. Final solution!"

I take a deep, painful breath. "Are you sure about this? Why aren't there headlines in the newspapers?"

Leona crushes the butt of her cigarette and exhales a

last puff. "Because, sweetie, people either don't want to believe it or they really don't care. Haven't you learned anything from Helga about hostility towards the Jews in Germany, in England, and even here where she's taken refuge?"

"Yes, but…do you really think Helga's father and mother and her sisters might become part of the…the 'Final Solution'? And does she even know about the poison gas and the ovens yet? It's too terrible to even imagine."

Leona shakes her head. "I know this sounds harsh, but her father may already have died from overwork, starvation, disease, torture, in the labor camp in Germany. And she hasn't heard from her mother or sisters in more than two years. Now there are transit camps in Holland from which captured Jews are sent to the gas ovens in Poland."

This discussion with Leona Simon is so horrifying that it's actually a relief when the apartment door opens and in walks Sibby. Her cheeks are flushed and she looks as if she's been running through the dark November streets.

Unlike my mother, Leona doesn't let go with a shrill demand for an immediate explanation. She simply lights a cigarette and looks at Sybil critically with darting, inquisitive eyes.

This is definitely the signal for me to get out of

there. Besides, my mother will be looking for me as well. "Thanks for...for having me," I tell Leona. "Our talk was so...interesting." Leona nods, but Sibby just glares at me. I can tell she's angry and that she's also suspicious as to what I've been discussing with her mother.

Well, guess what? I'm mad at her, too. Did she really think I had planned to dump her for Billy Crosby? I would never have done that in a million years if she hadn't walked out on me and left me no choice. If she doesn't know that, she's no kind of friend at all.

Growing more and more indignant as I go, I stomp up the two flights of stairs and down the long corridor to my own front door.

Mrs. Boylan, my seventh-grade history teacher, is a tall big-bosomed woman with—excuse me for saying it—a bulldoggy face.

"Yes, Isabel, did you have a question about the Third Crusade?"

It's Monday morning after the Thanksgiving weekend and nobody is really happy about returning to school. But, I, on the other hand, am full of enthusiasm because ever since Saturday there's something I've been anxious to talk about in history class that has nothing to do with the Middle Ages.

It's not about landlords and peasants, or nobles and vassals, or Christians and Muslims smashing each other to smithereens during the Crusades, of which there were at least four, if not more. As I see it, that all happened a long, long time ago and there's nothing anybody can do about it today.

"Not the Crusades," I announce, getting to my feet. "I know we're supposed to study the Middle Ages. But there's something happening in the world right now that not too many people know about and…and if they did maybe something could be done about it."

Mrs. Boylan looks at me with curiosity. I've never even raised my hand in class before.

"Do you mean the war, Isabel?"

"Well yes, in a way. It's…it's about the concentration camps the Nazis are building in Europe so they can gas the Jews and burn their bodies. It's called the 'Final Solution.' As I said, there's only a little being reported in the papers. We're just beginning to find out about it."

Mrs. Boylan gives me an almost pitying look. "Yes, well of course there have been atrocities committed by Hitler against all sorts of people. But what you suggest sounds extreme unless you have strong evidence to back it up. Why don't you bring in some newspaper clippings and do a special assignment on these concentration camps you talk about. I would give you extra credit, Isabel. And that would be very helpful toward your final grade."

I know this is the signal for me to say, *Yes, ma'am*, and sit down. But stubbornly I remain standing. "If you don't believe how terrible things are in Germany, there is a person in this very school who could tell you. The last she heard her father was in a prison camp called Buchenwald, although he's probably dead by now, and her mother and sisters…"

"Isabel dear," Mrs. Boylan breaks in, "I'm sure the class would like to hear more about this situation, but we really have a great deal to cover regarding the Third Crusade. We are mandated, you know, to teach the Middle Ages in seventh grade. It's part of the curriculum."

The eyes of every person in the class are on me as I grumpily take my seat. But who cares? Let them snicker and pass snide remarks among them. This is nothing compared to being threatened with a knifing by the Hitler Youth, sent away from your family forever on the Kindertransport, being stoned by English schoolchildren for being a Jew and hanging out with an "idiot."

For the rest of the period I keep my head down and refuse to even turn the pages of my textbook. What can Mrs. Boylan do to me? Throw me in jail, torture me, stuff me into an oven like the old witch in *Hansel and Gretel*? This is the U.S.A. It's a free country.

# Seventeen

"I heard," Sybil says, "that you got into trouble in Boylan's class."

Apparently, even though she and I walked to school separately this morning, she isn't as mad at me as she seemed to be on Saturday when she found me in her apartment talking to Leona.

But I'm still feeling pretty ticked off at her. "I didn't get into trouble," I reply icily. "I just asked a question. And got a stupid answer. It's not my fault if Mrs. Boylan prefers to be living during the Third Crusade and the kids in the class are a bunch of goofballs."

"Yeah," Sybil muses, "I heard you brought up something about the Nazis. You're getting even more like Leona than I am…"

It's just after last period and we're standing in the hall near the door of our homeroom, being elbowed by kids passing through. Also, any minute now Billy Crosby will be coming by and I don't want to get into another tangle with him and Sibby.

"Listen," I break in, "I've got a bone to pick with you.

And it's about Saturday. And you know why. If you want to walk home together after dismissal, we can talk about it then."

Sybil is waiting for me at the main gate looking even more apologetic than before.

I tell her about Helga, who isn't in school today because she's staying up in Westchester with Mrs. F. for a while longer. And then I let her have it about deserting me in front of Billy.

"I thought you *wanted* to be left alone with him," Sibby exclaims defensively. "Why don't you face it, Izzie? You like it that he's running after you."

"I don't, I don't. He tries to boss me around. He makes me feel…helpless."

"Well, then there must be something wrong with you. That's what girls are supposed to like. They want to be chased after. And finally captured."

"Do you?"

"How should I know? I haven't got a boyfriend."

"Please don't say that word," I implore Sibby. I can see that this conversation is getting us nowhere. "So," I say, "tell me what you really did on Saturday. You never went downtown all by yourself, did you?"

Sibby switches her books to her other arm and sighs. "I did. Thanks for not telling Leona."

"You did? What was it like? Did you get to see *Casablanca*?"

"Of course not. There was a line all the way around the block. Police all over the place, soldiers and sailors everywhere. You had to be eighteen to get in."

"So what did you do?"

"Walked around. Hung out near the big Broadway USO, the Stage Door Canteen on 44th Street, hoping I'd see some movie stars or famous singers. Bought myself an orangeade and a hot dog with mustard. A couple of sailors, really young-looking, called me "Red" and followed me for half a block."

"Hmm. Sounds like fun."

"It wasn't. It became sort of weird, even a little scary. So I got back on the subway and came home. Doing stuff alone isn't that much fun. Tell me about you and Billy."

It's a little over a year now since December 7, 1941, that terrible Sunday when the Japs bombed Pearl Harbor in far-off Hawaii. "Over two thousand Americans killed in surprise attack on naval base, ships and planes destroyed," my father read out loud from the newspaper. "A date which will live in infamy," said President Franklin D. Roosevelt. And in no time at all we were fighting the Japs, the Italians, and the Germans in World War II.

At first, the war didn't mean that much to me. I have to admit that I saw it as more of an inconvenience than anything else. So I'm actually surprised at how far I stuck my neck out in history class the other day.

Now there are notes on my desk and whispers in my ear every time I walk into Mrs. Boylan's room. "Hey, Isabel, heard anything from the concentration camps lately?"

"Psst, I think I just smelled some of that Nazi poison gas. Did you?"

Day by day, as we grope our way through the dark and dreary Middle Ages, I'm becoming more and more infuriated. I may not be able to convince Mrs. Boylan of Hitler's recently devised Final Solution, but I have pretty good evidence of how bad things already were in Nazi Germany in 1939 when Helga left.

So, for the second time this term, I raise my hand. Mrs. Boylan lifts her eyebrows and says, "Yes, Isabel. What is that you're holding up? If it's the special assignment we talked about, please leave it on my desk."

"No." I get to my feet. "It's something else. It's about the Jewish children in Germany who were sent to England to escape being killed by the Nazis. They left their families and probably will never see them again. It was called the Kindertransport."

I wave the paper I've been holding above my head. "This is a real-life story. If you don't believe it, there is a person in this school who was a Kindertransport child and she can swear to you that every word is true. The school ought to pay some attention to things like that, especially in history class."

Mrs. Boylan appears a little nonplussed, and the rest of the class is looking from the teacher to me and back, just waiting to see what is going to happen next.

"I'm sure this is very interesting and important, Isabel," Mrs. Boylan says, "and I'll be happy to read your paper and consider giving you extra credit for it. But, as far as taking up the Kindertransport in class, I think that might be a better subject for your homeroom teacher."

Mrs. Boylan does walk over to my desk, though, and I hand her Helga's story.

"I'd just like to mention something that explains why people were so scared in Germany that they sent their children away," I add. "It's in the report."

"Yes, Isabel?" I can tell Mrs. Boylan is getting impatient with me.

"It's the Hitler Youth marching song. They've been singing it for years and years, ever since Hitler took over Germany. It's sung in German, of course. But here's how it goes in English: *And when Jewish blood spurts from the knife, then things will again go well.*"

Mrs. Boylan returns to her desk. I take my seat. Nobody says a word.

"Now, boys and girls," Mrs. Boylan announces in her usual calm, teacherly voice, "open your history books to page 132, *The Lives of the Peasants and the Serfs on the Manor of the Lord.*"

Helga has been out of school now for a whole week. So I feel a little awkward going up to our homeroom teacher, Mr. Jeffers, to tell him that Mrs. Boylan thinks we should talk about the Kindertransport and other monstrous things that have gone on in Germany in his class instead of hers.

He's already asked me about Helga's absence and reminded me that after the third day he was supposed to have received a note. The Frankfurters said they were sending one, but it seems it hasn't arrived yet.

Sure enough, just before Friday dismissal, Mr. Jeffers beckons me to his desk. I wonder for a moment if he's had a message from Mrs. Boylan, putting the burden of the Kindertransport and the Final Solution on his shoulders. In a way, that would be very nice. At least, I'd finally be able to broadcast what I know and get some attention from the teachers and students at Simpleton Junior High.

But no...Mr. Jeffers just stares at me with his popping, panda-like eyes and says, "I have not as yet heard from Helga Frankfurter's guardians regarding her absence of one whole week. If she is still living at your address, Isabel, she's required to attend school in this district, and an attendance officer will be sent to your home without further delay."

Mr. Jeffers looks nervously around the room, which is becoming hooligan-like with Friday-afternoon hilarity. He clears his throat. "Of course, if on the other hand

Miss Frankfurter is planning to relocate her address, that becomes the responsibility of the school in that district."

"Oh," I say, bobbing my head up and down with certainty, "I'm sure Helga will be back in class on Monday."

Then an important thought connected with Helga's absence comes to me. "About her missing school this past week," I add, "I wouldn't get too excited. You know she didn't go to school in Germany for years because the Nazis burned down all the schools where the Jewish children were sent. Then, when she arrived in England as a refugee on the Kindertransport, the schoolchildren in the village threw stones at her for being Jewish. So she didn't go to school there either." I pause to let my message sink in. "Excuse me for asking, but what do you think of that, Mr. Jeffers?"

Mr. Jeffers' giraffe-like neck is about all I can see of him. His eyes are fixed on the boys at the back of the room, who are slamming books over each other's heads. Just above his shirt collar, Mr. Jeffers' Adam's apple appears to be working itself up and down faster and faster. Then he raises the yardstick in his hand. It goes flashing past me and comes down on the lip of his desk with a resounding smack.

I jump back in alarm.

Silence follows and Mr. Jeffers turns to me once again. Even though it's pretty chilly these December days, indoors as well as out—because the entire country is being asked to conserve coal for the war effort—Mr. Jeffers' ghostly face is coated with a sickly film of perspiration. As a teacher he's both stern and ill at ease, and it's hard not to feel uncomfortable with him. Yet I can't help feeling a little sorry for him. I've noticed that the boys in class act up a lot as a way of challenging him, probably because they suspect his draft card says 4-F, unfit for service.

"You were saying, Isabel…"

With that, the dismissal bell rings. Pandemonium breaks loose in the classroom again and everyone goes charging out. Even Mr. Jeffers, briefcase already clutched in his hand, appears to be on the run.

"Oh, nothing," I murmur. It's doubtful that he can even hear me over the din. "I'll, uh, tell Helga what you said…about bringing in an absence note on Monday."

It's Friday evening and I'm alone in the apartment, which has been feeling strangely empty anyhow this week without Helga. I poke around absently, going from room to room. I stare out the window. I turn the radio on and turn it off again.

The brush-off I got today from Mrs. Boylan about the Kindertransport has left me feeling totally frustrated. And then there was my failure to get Mr. Jeffers interested. I'm afraid that even if I can get his attention the next time I talk to him, he's not going to care much about the victims of the Nazis all over Europe who are doomed to be part of the Final Solution. He's much too busy trying to keep order in homeroom.

Stubborn thoughts keep nagging at me, though. Maybe I do have one more hope.

A couple of months ago, Mrs. Brody in English assigned an essay, *How My Life Has Changed Since Pearl Harbor*. I wrote about blackouts, rationing, turning in metal scrap and rubber, and even saving up cooking fats to be made into glycerin for explosives. I wrote about my brother enlisting in the Air Force and I wrote about Helga coming to live with us. But I hardly knew anything about her at the time, only that she was a refugee from Germany by way of England.

Now, I find myself haunted by the picture of Helga's family that I saw in the box marked *Schokoladen* that morning at Moskin's, when she went off on her pre-breakfast hike. I want to look again at her father and mother and their three little girls at a time when all of them were so much younger and life appeared to be carefree and happy.

And, if I took another look, what else might I find inside that box, aside from the letters written in German by Helga's *Mutti*? More photographs, Helga's picture as a Kindertransport child, other evidence of her life haunted by the Nazis?

If this is snooping, I tell myself…so be it. The reason for it is important. Suppose it could in some way save the lives of others.

I enter our bedroom, find the chocolate box easily (Helga hasn't even gone to much trouble to conceal it), sit down on my bed with it on my lap, and carefully raise the cover expecting to once again see the picture of Helga's family on top.

To my astonishment, a folded blue air letter flies out and gently floats to the floor. I snatch it up breathlessly. I can see at once that it's not one of Helga's many letters written in German, with a foreign stamp and postmark and addressed in polite, slanted penmanship. The handwriting is large and scrawling and the letter is addressed to Helga at her aunt and uncle's house in Westchester.

Roy! Even before my eye falls on the government post-office return address, which is now used to send mail to members of the armed forces, I know that the letter had to have arrived after Helga left Shady Pines. Most likely it was sent from the ship to which Roy was assigned for duty in the Pacific, after his furlough.

The envelope has a rough tear in it. Maybe Helga herself did this in the excitement of receiving the letter. Beyond the torn edge, a single page is begging to be unfolded.

But I absolutely must not and cannot do this. Finding the chocolate box so I can look for more pictures or other evidence of Helga's life in Germany is one thing. But reading a letter as private as this one is something I definitely must not…

And yet…and yet…

*Dear Sweet Helga,*

*So you're feeling better I hope. Boy, I can't forget the way you were crying that night, especially when we said goodbye. You told me it was because it was the first time you heard anyone speak your own language to you in three years.*

*So it reminded you of how much you missed your home and your family. Yeah, well like I told you, my grandmother raised me and she and I still speak the language when we're together. And that's how I keep in practice.*

*I can't tell you much about my life in the Navy. Censorship and all that, you know. But it's okay out here and I'm making some good pals. No women around, so you're perfectly safe, you sweet kid.*

*Sure hope things work out for you in your new life in the U.S. But you seemed so scared and not sure you would be able to stay with those people who brought you over. So remember what I told you if you ever get in any kind of trouble. I showed you where the key is hid.*

*Hey kid, I still don't believe that was your first kiss. How could anybody stay away from you? So be good, now. Close your eyes and think of me.*

*Roy*

# Eighteen

Two days later I'm still reeling from Roy's letter to Helga. It's bad enough that I went ahead and read it. But what does it all mean?

Well, it's pretty clear that they kissed. Only once? More? Also, it partly explains Helga's tears, even after she came back to our room that night and pretended to be asleep. But what did Helga tell Roy about her fears and uncertainties? Why, at that time, was she afraid she wouldn't be able to stay with Mr. and Mrs. F.?

"Isabel, are you ready? Sybil is here." My mother's voice breaks into my dithering thoughts and I rush out of my room, still panicky with guilt. No one must ever know that I read that letter. No one, not Sibby, not my parents, and most of all, not Helga.

I hardly know how I can face Helga later this afternoon, when we're driving up to Westchester to bring her home after her week with Mr. and Mrs. F. and her absence from school. Is that why I insisted that Sybil be invited to come along?

"It's only going to be a short visit," my mother

reminded me when she finally agreed to take Sybil with us. "Don't even think about ice skating or horseback riding or any of those things Harriette Frankfurter mentioned when she was here at Thanksgiving. Her situation is very grave now, so this isn't a social call."

Sibby has gotten pretty dressed up, though, almost as though she's going to a party. I guess it's because she's heard so much about the Frankfurters' elegant and spacious house set back on sweeping lawns and surrounded by tall handsome trees. Right now there's snow on the ground, so the place probably looks like a fairyland, and I won't blame Helga if she's sorry to leave.

We've had snow in the Bronx, too, as I once promised her. But the streets here look awful. The curbs are heaped with frozen mounds and high ridges of grimy, frozen stuff, the color of filthy rags, and the sidewalks are covered with sprawling patches of ice.

Sibby and I sit quietly in the back seat while my parents discuss the latest news from my brother Arnold, who has written that he's about to be shipped out but he still doesn't know where. My mother insists he's going to the Pacific to be shot down by the Japanese the first time he takes off from an aircraft carrier. "Then, we'll find out what really happened to those 'heroes' of the Doolittle raids back in April," she says bitterly.

"Don't get hysterical, Sally," my father advises her, as he steers the car through the snow-banked streets toward the outer reaches of the city. "The boy hasn't even been in an airplane yet. I say they're sending him to England for his flight training. You'll see that I'm right. I can just read between the headlines. That boy will be dropping bombs over Germany one of these days. Mark my word."

Sibby flashes me a look and I flash one back. "You're so quiet, Izzie," she remarks softly, as my parents continue their barrage of one another. "Is it about Helga? Don't you want her to come back?"

"Of course I do. Why do you think I've been working so hard on the teachers at school? Once Helga's back in class, maybe I can get them to let her tell her story."

"If she'll talk. Remember how worried she is about her family."

"She'll talk. Sooner or later, she's got to hear about the Final Solution. And she's just the person to sound a wake-up call at Simpleton."

But when Helga herself opens the door for us at the Frankfurter house, I can hardly envision her as the fearless spokesperson against Hitlerism that I've been grooming her to be. She has deep circles under her eyes, her face is expressionless, and she hardly seems glad to see us. The house behind her is hushed, except for Mr. F. who comes forward murmuring softly and immediately takes my parents off to another room.

"Are you okay, Helga?" I ask anxiously. "You don't

look well."

There's a long pause as the three of us stand awkwardly in the entrance hall. At last Helga speaks. "She is dying."

"What?" Sibby and I exchange terrified glances.

"Aunt Harriette is dying. It is only a matter of days, perhaps hours."

I grab Helga by the shoulders. "Where is she?"

Helga waves a finger over her shoulder, indicating a rear portion of the house.

"Why isn't she in the hospital?" Sybil nods in approval of my question.

"There is nothing that can be done for her. She has cancer. There is a private nurse with her for medicine to relieve the pain." Helga turns away from us briefly. "Oh, I am sorry. Come in. I will show you upstairs to my bedroom."

We walk through the living room with its bright carpets and softly toned rich woods, a reflection of Mrs. F.'s tastes and her preference for pleasing earth colors. There is a cozy-looking den with bookshelves and a fireplace off to one side. We follow Helga up a curving polished staircase to the floor above and past several doorways to her own room  It's charmingly decorated in flowered chintz and white organdy without being too frilly.

"Wow," Sibby exclaims. "This house is gorgeous. You are so lucky to…" Her words come to an abrupt halt and she claps the back of her hand to her mouth.

"Sit down, please," Helga says, without appearing to react to Sybil's inappropriate remark. Helga indicates a pair of white wicker chairs with flowered seat cushions.

I remain standing at the window, looking down at the snow-covered shrubs in the garden below. I've been to the Frankfurters' house before, with my parents. But this time there is so much to absorb. How could Harriette Frankfurter, of all people, be dying? Only a few months ago at Moskin's, she was her bright and peppy self, color-fully and attractively dressed, brimming with energy, and patiently—ever so patiently—trying to teach me to knit.

"Maybe," I say hesitantly as I slip into one of the pretty chairs, "she is only going through a bad spell, a…a crisis. You hear about these amazing recoveries."

Helga is sitting stiffly on the side of her bed. "No, no. I am sorry, Isabel. There is no use lying to me."

Helga's use of the word lying makes me feel like I've been stabbed. The things I've done to Helga fill me with guilt. I've envied her, snooped around among her personal belongings, resented her coming to live with us, read her letter from Roy…

"Well, you still have a home with us," I say as warmly and reassuringly as I can. "It was really lonely this week without you, Helga. And there was stuff happening at school that I…I needed you for."

"Also," Sibby breaks in, "Izzie had a date with Billy Cros-by. He bought her a cherry Coke. Can you believe that?"

I give Sibby a look. "Helga's not interested in that kind of kid stuff." I turn to Helga. "It wasn't a date. It was just a dumb coincidence. It was Sybil's fault really."

What in the world are we doing talking about nonsense like this, while downstairs Mrs. F. is lying in bed, drugged with medicines to ease the pain of the disease that is killing her?

I lean toward Helga, still sitting almost zombie-like on the bed. "What will you do? You will come back to us, won't you, Helga? I mean, after, um…"

"After Aunt Harriette dies? No, I cannot. It is not right that other people should care for me…perhaps for years and years. This is impossible for me to accept."

"So you'll stay here, then," Sibby remarks, looking around the room admiringly. "I guess you could live here with your uncle, go to school here, make friends. Of course, it's a big house for just the two of you, but…"

My mother suddenly appears in the doorway of Helga's room. "Ah, so this is where you three are hiding out. It was so quiet downstairs. Isabel, please come with me. I have to talk to you."

Now what have I done? I get up and follow my mother into the corridor and down the long, graceful staircase. At the bottom of the steps she turns to me. "Harriette Frankfurter wants to see you. I'll take you to her room. But I have to warn you, Isabel, that she is very ill. Don't stay long and don't jabber. Do you hear me?"

Trembling, I walk behind my mother as far as an alcove that leads to a ground-floor bedroom suite. The door is slightly ajar and a white-uniformed nurse invites me in. As I enter, she whispers, "Our patient's a bit sleepy but alert, so I'll leave you two alone. There's the bell if you need me." Then she circles around me and disappears out the door.

I've never been alone with a dying person before. Only a little over a week ago, Mrs. F. was sitting at our Thanksgiving table drinking champagne. True, she looked thin and peaked, and my final glimpse of her as the elevator door closed was of someone who was in pain and trying to conceal it.

But when I glance at the face of the person who is propped up on the pillow before me, I can't believe that this is the same Mrs. F. Only her voice and the words she uses—"Isabel darling, how wonderful to see you"—assure me that she is truly the woman I've known.

Her face is of the palest ivory. Her eyes, naked now of the eyeliner that always circled them, are mere sunken dots. Her once-full lips are parched-looking, her nose and chin sharply etched.

Even so she manages a faint smile.

"I look a fright. I wanted to put on make-up today but I was out of it most of the morning. Oh, it's lovely, Isabel, when the pain goes away for a while, and then I don't care at all. Not about anything. Isn't that remarkable?"

I'm sitting on a chair beside the bed. I've never felt so tongue-tied in all my life.

But, as usual, Harriette Frankfurter takes over in an attempt to make it easier for me. "I wanted to see you, Isabel, to thank you for everything you've done for Helga, for being so welcoming and so helpful, for being such a good roommate, above all for being such a marvelous friend to her right from the start."

I begin to shake my head. "No, no."

"Don't tell me it's nothing. Not everyone would have been so loyal and so caring as you've been, from the very moment she first arrived at Shady Pines, a complete stranger to you."

How can I stop Mrs. F. from going on with these undeserved compliments? Disloyal and dishonest acts I've committed race through my mind…from that first morning when I peered into Helga's chocolate box to two days ago when I read Roy's letter.

There were so many other things, too…my envy of the attention paid to Helga at Moskin's, how mad I was when she ended up with the dungarees I couldn't fit into, my tattling to both Ruthie and Sibby about the night Helga sneaked out with Roy. Was I caring? Ha. Was I loyal? Hardly.

I'm still trying to think of a way to denounce myself, to explain to Mrs. F. that, when it comes to Helga, I've been far from a model friend, when she utters a small, thin shriek. "Oh, my dear," she says in a suddenly stressed voice, "I think the pain is returning."

But before I can get up to call the nurse, she grips my arm. "No, not just yet. There's more. It's about Helga. Herman has recently found out that his brother Josef, Helga's father, died some time ago in Buchenwald, where he was deliberately shot to death. Her mother and two sisters, having been smuggled into Holland, have now disappeared entirely. Herman believes they were discovered by the Dutch Nazis and sent to one of the extermination camps. Martina, you know, was guilty of having married a Jew and produced "crossbreed" children.

"But we've been afraid to tell Helga because something terrible is gnawing away at her. She is riddled with guilt. She doesn't feel she should have been given a chance to survive. I'm very worried about…"

Mrs. F. winces and this time her shriek of pain is much louder. I jump to my feet to ring the bell for the nurse. Probably she has been waiting behind the partly open door because she's already in the room. I turn to say goodbye to Mrs. F. and, although only an instant has passed, her eyes are closed and her face looks like a mask.

Words pass silently from my lips. *Goodbye, goodbye, darling Mrs. F.* Then I feel my mother's hands on my elbows, guiding me from the room. As usual I'm expecting a scolding. I stayed too long. I talked too much.

I wore Harriette Frankfurter out. If she dies as this very moment, it's my fault.

But no, my mother doesn't say a word. She directs me toward the front of the house, where my father and Sibby are already getting into their hats and coats. But where is Helga and the small suitcase she took with her when she left us at Thanksgiving?

My question is answered when Helga appears in the front hall with Mr. F. She isn't dressed to leave and there's no sign of her luggage. Mr. F., always so quiet and agreeable to almost everything, seems agitated. The three grownups look at each other helplessly. Apparently there's already been a fair amount of discussion about the fact that Helga refuses to go back home to the Bronx with us.

"When it is the right time," Helga says with amazing authority for someone who's always been so soft-spoken and polite, "I take the railroad from here to you. I have a timetable for all the trains. I know what is the correct route to follow to the Grand Central Station and then on the subway. I am not such, as you say, a ninny."

"Why Helga dear," my mother exclaims, "nobody ever thought you were a 'ninny.' I can understand your wanting to stay with your aunt until the very end. It's just that it will be so hard for you and so lonely here. It…it isn't a very good atmosphere for a young girl who's already been through as much as you have."

"And," I cut in, "you'll be missing a lot of school. It's still a couple of weeks until Christmas." I get a bright thought. "You could go home with us now and then, when the vacation starts, come back…"

My mother taps me hard on the shoulder. I guess this is a dumb idea. How do we know Mrs. F. is going to live until Christmas? My trying to persuade Helga to come home with us now is probably more for my sake than hers, because I'm so racked with guilt toward her—more so than ever since my talk with Mrs. F.

We drive home in silence, each of us afraid—I suspect—to open our mouths and say the wrong thing in the awesome presence of approaching death.

Surely my mother is thinking of her long friendship with Harriette Frankfurter. They met in school when they were Sibby's and my age and have been close ever since. My father, on the other hand, is probably still focusing on his fantasy of Arnold, triumphantly flying a bomber one of these days over Nazi Germany.

Sibby, I'd guess, is mulling over the beauty and comfort of the sad house in Westchester, so different from her family's spare apartment in the Bronx.

And me…I'm still trying to puzzle out that next-to-last paragraph of Roy's letter to Helga.

# Nineteen

Sibby and I are in Hansen's drugstore shopping for Christmas cards. "Stop looking around," Sibby orders. "Just because he brought you here for a Coke a couple of weeks ago doesn't mean you're still going to find him sitting at the soda fountain."

"I'm not talking to you," I snap. "I wasn't even looking in that direction. What do you think of this card for Mrs. Boylan? Is it cold and icy enough?"

I don't know why we do this, but every year we buy Christmas cards to give to our teachers unless we absolutely, positively know that they are Jewish and definitely wouldn't like the idea. We always used to buy presents for them, too. But junior high, with a different teacher for each subject, makes that awfully expensive.

I would like to get something for Miss Damore, though. So after we finish up with the cards we go to the perfume counter and start sniffing the sample bottles.

"Which of these do you think smells more French?" I ask Sibby, spraying her with a little of each. "*Evening in Paris* or *Nuit d'Amour*?"

Sybil backs away, but not fast enough. "They both stink," she says, waving her hands wildly in the air. "Leona says soap and water are the best perfume and a whole lot cheaper. Anyhow, don't the names mean the same thing?"

"Not at all. *Nuit d'Amour* doesn't mean 'Evening in Paris'; it means 'Night of Love.'"

"Oh, I see…a whole night of love all over France, not just an evening in Paris. Better get that one. It seems like more for the money."

Even though it costs a dollar over what I was planning to spend, I buy the fancy crystal purse-size bottle of *Nuit d'Amour*. I wonder if Billy Crosby will even think of getting a gift for Miss Damore.

On the way out, I can't help stopping to admire the Christmas-tree decorations. The prettiest of the fragile, colored glass balls glazed with silvery sparkles always used to come from Japan, along with China dolls, toy tea sets, and, of course, anything made of silk—pajamas, negligees, and sheer stockings. Now, of course, there are no Japanese imports aside from hand grenades and bombs being delivered to our troops all over the Pacific. And I don't really know why I care about Christmas decorations because we never have a Christmas tree. As my father says, "It's against our religion."

Still, it's hard to keep from getting excited about the Christmas season. We're singing carols in school assembly and the classrooms are decorated with pictures of Santa

Claus, red and green streamers, and Christmas wreaths, all of which is very confusing.

Even more confusing are the busy shopping streets, when Sibby and I emerge from Hansen's with our modest packages. Even though there are shortages of so many gift items this year, from waffle irons to cocktail shakers, from rubber galoshes to ice skates, Christmas lures passersby into the stores.

At the same time, reminders of the war are all around us. Signs with patriotic mottos mingle with the holiday tinsel—"V for Victory!"; "Win the War, Help the Boys"; "Uncle Sam Needs You."

Today was a school day, only one more day to go before Christmas vacation begins, so it's already dark out when I softly turn my key in the door of the apartment. If my mother is home I'll show her the cards I bought for my teachers. But should I also show her the coat-lapel ornament I bought, which I just couldn't resist—a little snowman wreathed in miniature red berries and holding a tiny bell that actually tinkles.

Sibby bought one, too. "Leona won't mind, but what about your mom? You have to admit, it is sort of Christmassy."

"It's not," I insisted, carefully examining my trinket as I paid for it at the counter. "It's wintry. That's all it is, a symbol of the winter season."

My mother's voice calls out from the bedroom. "Isabel, is that you?"

She's home after all. But why are there so few lights on, and why is there such an air of exceptional quiet in the apartment? Before I can reach my parents' room, my mother comes toward me, a handkerchief clutched in her hand.

"Oh."

I know at once that the news we've all been dreading has come.

"Harriette Frankfurter passed away this afternoon," my mother says in a doleful voice. I can tell that she's been weeping. "I'm waiting for your father. We're going up to Westchester to help with funeral arrangements. I think you should stay at Sybil's this evening if it's all right with her mother."

I knew that Mrs. F. was dying when I last saw her, but this is a shock. Although the world is full of death these days, with the war on—and more and more gold stars appearing in people's windows—I haven't ever really been close to anybody who died. What is it like to say goodbye to someone forever? Will I have to go to the funeral? Will I have to see Mrs. F. in her coffin?

"No, of course, Sybil can't go. What's happened to you, Isabel? Are you using Sybil as a crutch? Aren't you thinking at all about Helga? It's your duty to be supportive of her at a terrible time like this," my mother reminds me.

It's early Sunday, two days after Christmas, and the morning of Harriette Frankfurter's funeral, which is to take place at a cemetery not far from the home of Mr. and Mrs. F.

First, however, we go to the funeral-home chapel where there will be a service conducted by a rabbi. People, sad-eyed and dressed in somber colors, arrive in great numbers and stand around whispering to one another in grave tones. Mr. F. is surrounded by men and women offering their condolences. My father explains to my mother that many of them are business acquaintances who have come with their wives to pay their respects. There are also neighbors and friends, but not many relatives because Mr. F. left Germany many years ago and Mrs. F. came from a very small family.

I stand beside Helga, who lingers at the fringe of the crowd, looking out of place and uncomfortable. From time to time, people approach her and say, "Ah, so you're the niece who Herman Frankfurter brought over from Europe. So sorry for your loss, dear."

Helga just nods and says, "Thank you."

"I guess you don't know many people here," I comment sympathetically

"I know nobody," Helga says with an unusually bitter edge to her voice. "These are all strangers. Everywhere people are strangers."

I nudge her arm in a show of solidarity. "Well, we're not. You aren't alone, Helga. You're coming home with us right after the funeral. I hope you packed everything."

In deep solemn voices, attendants in black suits now request that everyone file into the chapel for the service. Men who are not already wearing skullcaps are offered the round black head-coverings, in keeping with the laws of the Jewish religion. The few females who have come to the funeral hatless are given small black head veils. Helga is among them.

I'm walking next to Helga behind a slow-moving group of mourners, when another man in a black suit pulls her away from me. "Family members in the first pew. Family members only."

I look around. My parents, already seated a few pews back, are beckoning to me. My mother hisses in a stage whisper, "Where were you going?"

I slide in beside my parents. "You told me to stay with Helga. I don't know the rules around here. I was only following the crowd."

"God forbid," my father explains in a more patient manner than usual, "you should sit in the first row."

"It's bad luck?"

"Sure it's bad luck. It means you've lost someone close to you, a family member by either blood or marriage."

How stupid I am. Suddenly I'm returned to the reality of why we are here. What with the hubbub and the anxiety of trying to behave correctly in this strange place, I've almost completely forgotten about poor Mrs. F.

And now my eye lights on the burnished wooden coffin that rests on a bier at the front of the chapel, where the chief mourners are seated. Sadly, there are only two—Mr. F., his balding head covered with a black skullcap, and Helga, whose long honey-brown hair glimmers beneath its gauzy veil in the subdued light of the chapel.

My eye returns to the coffin. Is it forbidden, I wonder, to think of what Mrs. F. looks like lying beneath its closed lid? I'd like to imagine that she has her eyeliner on once again, that her scarlet lipstick and matching rouge are applied with as fine a touch as always, that her coppery hair is curled to perfection. And that she is wearing something lovely from her well-chosen wardrobe.

A hush settles over the crowd and the rabbi begins the service. He is black-bearded and stern. He speaks of Harriette Frankfurter as "the departed" and as a "good and righteous woman," which could be anybody and doesn't tell you the least little thing about her. The rest of what he says is mainly in Hebrew, which I don't understand, and is interrupted by chanting and by several requests for those present to rise.

Then it's one of the "black suits" again, up at the podium, giving instructions to all of those present that are planning to "attend the interment." They will follow the hearse, with their headlights on, to the cemetery gate and then on to the gravesite.

I glance questioningly at my parents. Must I really see Mrs. F., in her lovely shining coffin, lowered into the earth? Perhaps, I think to myself, I could just wait around here and be picked up later on the way home.

But one return look from my mother and I know the answer…Helga. I'm expected to be there for Helga, Helga who suffers so many woes, and whose sorrows I am obliged to witness and to support as a penalty, I suppose, for my own good fortune.

Of all things, we seem to be having a party at the home of Mr. and Mrs. F. on our return from the cemetery. The house is cheerfully lit, after the chill and the early winter darkness of the burial ground. Two hired servants as well as the housekeeper of Mr. and Mrs. F. have set a laden buffet table.

Ice cubes clink in glasses as cocktails and highballs are poured. Salty smoked fish, cheeses, eggs, salads, and fresh rolls are the main fare. This is a custom that Helga says she is not familiar with. My mother explains that the funeral foods are symbolic of both the tears that are shed (the salty fish) and the renewal of life (the eggs).

Smoked fish isn't exactly to my taste. But there is also an array of cakes, pastries, and cookies. After the horror of watching Mrs. F.'s coffin lowered into her open grave and covered by each mourner with a shovelful of raw earth, I need to drown myself in as much sweetness as I can stand. So I concentrate on the dessert table, helping myself to baby cream puffs and eclairs the size of a pinkie finger, jam tarts and nut pastries, buttery cookies dipped in thick chocolate. Where does Mr. F. get such luxuries during wartime?

After a while, the dining room gets extremely noisy, so I retreat with my cache of goodies to the cozy den off the living room, with its lit fireplace and book-lined walls. Some of my favorite authors are here...Louisa May Alcott, Charles Dickens, Mark Twain...including titles that I haven't read yet. I wonder if I could ask to borrow a few.

Contentedly I sip my lemonade, munch on a delectable pastry layered with flecks of chocolate, and stare into the fire. The war that is raging throughout the world seems very far away. Even the most dreadful moments at the cemetery—the black-bearded rabbi's droning voice, the slowly sinking coffin, the clods of earth landing on its polished surface—are beginning to recede in memory into little more than a bad dream. And the fire, with its leaping licks of flame, is so mesmerizing that I slump back against the cushions, my eyelids growing heavy.

I have no idea how long I've been here half-stupe-fied, half-asleep before the fire. Voices, though, seem to be coming closer. "Where is she? I haven't seen her for a while now. Probably she's in here. The child must be so worn out."

I look up into the face of one of the strange women I remember seeing in the funeral parlor. The person she seems to have been discussing me with is my mother, who is standing beside her.

"Oh, sorry." I stretch and yawn, thrusting my arms above my head. "Here I am. Are we leaving now?"

"Isabel," my mother says with a slightly irritated twist of her head. "We were not looking for you. But get up anyway because we'll be heading for home very soon. Where's Helga?"

"Helga?" I sit up straighter. "How should I know? The last time I saw her she was talking to some people in the dining room. I think she was eating a hard-boiled egg."

My mother exchanges glances with the other woman and tsk-tsks.

"What? I stayed with her all through the burial part, which by the way was horrible and made everybody feel just terrible. There should have been some other way…"

"Stop it this instant," my mother orders "You're positively rude. I'm completely ashamed of you. Now go and find Helga this minute."

"Really!" I answer back, as I get to my feet. "I'm not her keeper." I don't mean to sound nasty toward Helga, but my mother's nagging always makes me surly.

I drag myself up the stairs to the second floor. My

stomach is starting to feel queasy and my legs are wobbly. All those sweet, whipped-creamy pastries seem to have done a job on my digestion. "Helga," I call out, as I approach her bedroom at the end of the corridor, "it's time to leave now. Are you ready?"

The bedroom door is closed. I knock softly at first and then a little louder. Maybe Helga, too, has dozed off. But there's no answer and, on instinct, I toss polite behavior to the winds and throw open the door.

The bed is neatly made and the ruffled curtains hang gracefully. Helga's bureau drawers and her closet are empty, so it's obvious she's already packed her suitcase and has probably taken it down the back stairs, the ones that the housekeeper uses.

I check the other upstairs rooms, all of which appear to be empty, and limp back down to the main floor, definitely suffering now from a whopping bellyache. How right Helga was to have eaten only one hard-boiled egg, if even that.

I advise my mother that Helga is on her way down. Then I head for the nearest bathroom and lock myself in.

# Twenty

I've only been in the bathroom a short time, rinsing my face with cold water and—happily—not being sick after all, when there's a loud knocking at the door. "Isabel, let me in."

It's my mother. I expect her to be furious with me because I've made a pig of myself. But she doesn't seem interested. Her expression instead is one of alarm.

"It's Helga," she says, slightly out of breath. "You said she was on her way downstairs. But we can't find her anywhere. Herman Frankfurter and your father have been searching the house from cellar to attic. Some of the men are outside now checking the grounds. We're thinking of calling the police. Do you know anything at all about this?"

"Me? I told you. She packed all her stuff. Not a thing was left in her room. What... Oh, you mean?"

"Isabel, please pay attention. This is serious, very serious. Helga is missing."

I cringe inwardly with a pang of shame and guilt. I know the last words that Mrs. F. spoke to me about

Helga—*Something terrible is gnawing away at her...she doesn't feel she should have been given a chance to survive.* I know certain mysterious and perplexing things that Helga has said to me during the months I've spent with her—*It is right that I should be punished...there is a lie that I will pay for all my life.* And I know the puzzling words that Roy has written to Helga, revealing thoughts she expressed to him that evening at Shady Pines—*You seemed so scared and not sure you would be able to stay with those people...I showed you where the key is hid.*

But I have never been able to put these bits and pieces together into a meaningful picture. Nor must anyone ever, ever know that I read Roy's letter. Yet, because of what I have learned about Helga, I must take action. Slowly, slowly, a fuzzy plan begins to take shape in my mind.

It's a dark December morning, shortly before dawn. My parents refused to leave yesterday without Helga. So the three of us remained overnight at the home of Mr. F.

Hour upon hour I've been lying uneasily in Helga's bed in the perfect bedroom with the frilled curtains and the white wicker furniture. It's impossible to sleep with the knowledge that Helga has vanished. Late into the night the police searched the neighborhood for her. They tracked the streets in and around the center of town and the nearby parks. They made inquiries at the railroad station, from which trains run into Manhattan's Grand Central Terminal.

That is the way Helga would have traveled if she had decided to take the train from Westchester to New York City. But why would Helga have done that, when she knew we were about to drive her home?

At last I've decided what I'm going to do. I dress as quietly as I can, creep down the stairs, and let myself out the front door into the bleak cold of an early Monday morning. It's a ten-minute walk to the railway station. But I get there in about seven, running to get out of view of the Frankfurter house as quickly as possible and also to keep from freezing. In my New York City Sunday-best winter coat and hat, I'm not exactly dressed for extended outdoor activity.

Even though it's so early, a mixture of weekday commuters and of servicemen—who are forever on the move these days—are also heading for the station. When I get there, the open-air platform is half-filled with waiting passengers.

There's a coal fire burning in the pot-bellied stove in the station office, and the welcoming warmth envelops me as I step up to the ticket window. The clerk behind the window is a stout woman in a green eye-shade and a heavy wool sweater. She's probably doing war work, having taken the job of a male station clerk who's off to the service.

"Y-e-e-s, young lady?"

My voice is creaky. I'm still out of breath from running. "Um, if I wanted to go to Harpers Falls from here, how would I do it?"

"Now ain't that funny? Was somebody in here yesterday just before I went off duty, asked me the same question. Young lady a bit older 'n you. Don't get many folks heading for Harper's Falls in the winter. Something going on up there?"

My heart leaps. Suddenly I don't feel the least bit guilty that I read Roy's letter. *I showed you where the key is hid.*

I have just about enough money to pay for a one-way train ticket and I'm given instructions to change from the main line to the branch line at a place called Highwater Junction. The next train is due at 6:08. I buy a crumb bun and a small container of milk at the food counter and sit anxiously on a wooden bench near the hot stove.

The northbound express is almost completely filled with servicemen, soldiers on their way, most likely, to one of the upstate training camps. If I were with Sibby, or even Ruthie, I guess we'd consider this a fascinating experience. As it is, though, I feel shy and uncomfortable.

"Where ya goin', sis?"

The soldier on the seat beside me has rosy cheeks and his skin is so smooth that I doubt if he even shaves yet.

Still, I feel uneasy talking to him. My plan has to remain totally secret. I'm making this wild journey purely on a hunch. I could be so wrong. I could get into so much trouble.

"Upstate," I tell him hesitantly, "to visit a friend."

"Hear they've got some snow up there." He gazes down at my "dress" shoes, flat-heeled black pumps with straps. "Better get yourself some boots before you go trekkin' around the countryside."

I really don't want to continue this conversation. I have entirely too much on my mind. So I don't ask him where's he's from or anything about his family. Although I'm sympathetic to everyone who's in the service, and I think of Arnold every time I see a uniform, I don't feel up to acting like a friendly USO hostess at the moment.

By the time I've changed trains at Highwater Junction and gotten off at the Harper's Falls station, it's late morning. Sure enough, it's been snowing up here. The countryside is blanketed in white, I can't tell how deep. But most of the streets in town are passable.

At least I've gotten this far and I know where I'm going next.

The house is exactly as I remember it from two or three seasons ago, when we were at Moskin's and had occasion to come into town. "Here's where I live in the winter," Ruthie had said. "My mom and I are downstairs, my aunt and uncle and their kids on the second floor."

I mount the steps to the broad wooden porch with its twin doorways. The door on the left, I recall, is Ruthie's. The one on the right leads to the upstairs apartment. I take a deep breath and say a prayer as I press the stained brass door bell. Suppose Ruthie's gone somewhere for Christmas vacation. We've only exchanged two letters since last summer. If she is here, she'll be completely surprised. Will she even be glad to see me?

Moment pass…I stamp my feet in the cold. The door starts to open slowly, cautiously. Then Ruthie's beloved moon face appears, gray eyes, short-cut taffy-brown hair. Before she can react, I throw my arms around her and scream her name.

"Isabel!" Ruthie cries out. "Izzie, what are you doing here?" She peers around beyond me toward the street. "Your folks?"

"Uh-uh. I'm alone. I came on the train. Ruthie, you have to help me. It's about Helga."

How different everything looks here in winter, especially to someone like me who's strictly a city person. We've already walked the half-mile to Shady Pines, the hotel shuttered and lonely-looking in the gray-white landscape, its shade trees bare and only the grim, towering evergreens on view.

Ruthie has supplied me with knee-high boots,

an extra sweater, and a knitted wool scarf and cap. We crunch along on the newly fallen snow, past the entrance to Shady Pines and beyond it to the road that curves away from the lake toward the summer bungalows that are hidden in the surrounding woods.

"So," Ruthie muses, "let me get this straight. You're sure that Helga bought a ticket for Harper's Falls at the railroad station yesterday. And the reason she did it was so she could disappear from the world by hiding out in Roy's family's summer cottage?"

I flap my arms against my body, as a stiff wind comes whooshing at us off the icy lake. "Yes."

"Excuse me for saying it. But that's crazy. Did she ever even see the bungalow colony? It has maybe twelve or fifteen cottages. How would she even know which one was Roy's?"

"Sure she could have seen it. When that dog bit her over near Roy's place, he borrowed a car from one of his neighbors to take her to the doctor. So afterward he returned the car. That gave him a chance to show her the cottage. Then he walked Helga back to the hotel."

"I still can't imagine her picking a place like this to run off to in the middle of winter. How long does she think she can hold out?"

"I told you, Ruthie. Helga is just not thinking right. She runs away from anybody who wants to take care of her. Not because she hates people...because she hates herself. Gosh, from here the lake looks like it's frozen solid. Do people go skating on it?"

"Uh-uh, not this early in the season," Ruthie cautions. "It's only December."

"Well, the weather feels cold enough to me," and I start walking faster as we enter the woods. I figure we're probably not far now from the spot where I tumbled to the ground after thinking I'd spotted a rustling snake, and where Roy found me and helped me up. So it can't be much of a distance to the bungalow colony itself.

Ruthie is panting behind me. "Hold up, Izzie. You're going the wrong way. There's a turn in the path here."

"How can you tell? Everything's covered with snow."

"Ah," Ruthie smiles. "That's why I'm a country girl and you're a city girl." And she starts walking ahead of me with an occasional look back and a grin.

Sure enough, after tramping through the woods for a while, I can make out the first of the cabins, painted dark green with white shutters. The cabins would be hard to spot in the summer among leafy surroundings, but they stand out clearly against the snowy background.

I'm filled with nervous anticipation as we start investigating one cabin after another. We tramp through the snow, knocking at the doors and trying to peer into the shuttered windows. But every single cottage appears to be locked and vacant, and a ghostly stillness lies all around us.

"I'm awfully afraid," Ruthie remarks with a patient but practical air, "that you and I are on a wild goose chase, Izzie."

Deep down, I'm almost ready to agree when, as we're approaching the eighth or ninth of the cottages, she suddenly thrusts out her arm as a signal for me to come to a dead stop.

Obediently, I remain stock still behind Ruthie. "What?"

"Don't take another step, Izzie. Look."

"Where?"

"Down. Look at the ground directly in front of you."

I can just make out the disturbances in the snow to which Ruthie is pointing. "Footprints?"

"Yes, boot marks. *Leaving* the cabin. If they're Helga's she may have come out after the snow stopped. And gone…"

"Where?"

Ruthie suddenly grabs my arm so hard I spin around. "Stay right behind me. From here on we walk in single file. Don't take even a tiny step on your own. I think I can follow these prints."

"To?"

"To the shortcut to the lake."

Peering anxiously through the bare trees as we approach the lake shore, I keep telling myself that Helga has to be here, somewhere, in this wintry desolation. It is so exactly the bleak and lonely setting she would choose in her distracted state of mind. I don't even know if Helga is in control of herself anymore. All I know is that time is passing and I need to find her...soon.

"Look!" Ruthie's eyes are sharper than mine. I forget my marching orders and rush up to where Ruthie is standing, on the bare shoreline. Far out on the lake, a figure is flitting gracefully on the ice, forming lazy circles and figure-eights, moving with ease and lightness and complete indifference.

"Oh, no!" I shout hoarsely.

The next moment Ruthie and I are both cupping our mouths and bawling her name. "H-e-l-g-a. H-e-l-g-a."

But Helga doesn't respond. She turns away, does a jump, whirls around again. I know that she skated a lot as a little girl in Germany, and I can see that she's good on the ice. But does she know how thinly frozen this lake is?

"Doesn't she see us?" Ruthie asks with a desperate air. "What's wrong with her?"

"She's acting really strange, Ruthie. I'm going after her."

"Oh no, you don't." Ruthie, usually so placid and always polite, tugs hard at my sleeve. "You could both go through the ice. I told you the lake isn't safe yet."

I tear free of Ruthie's grip. I've come this far and I'm not letting Helga go now. I know I haven't the power to pull her back to shore, but maybe once I get closer and can talk to her she'll listen to me.

"Izzie, be careful. Watch out for thin spots," Ruthie pleads from the shore, her voice growing fainter as I step out onto the lake with it's thin covering of recent snow. The ice beneath is rough and edgy in some places, smooth in others. I don't know which parts of the surface are safer to walk on.

As I get closer to Helga, I realize that I do have her attention. But she simply lifts both arms and waves me away.

"Helga," I cry out, "don't do this. Don't run away from me. I have to talk to you. Please, please come closer." On skates, I might actually be able to catch up to her. But in my clumsy boots, I stumble along, slipping and sliding, as I try to move faster and at the same time keep my balance.

"Helga, Helga!" Suddenly I'm sprawled on the ice. The snow-sprinkled patch where I've fallen is so smooth that I manage only briefly to get to my feet and then fall down hard again with a resounding thud. I lie there stunned, unable for the moment to even crawl on my belly. When I look up, a slender figure is looming above me.

"Oh, Helga, thank goodness. Why wouldn't you listen to me before? How could you run away like this? Do you know how worried everybody is about you?"

But even as Helga helps me to my feet, she remains stony-faced and says nothing.

"Helga, answer me. You're making me really angry now. No matter what troubles you have, you still have to talk to me. Answer me, why won't you?"

Helga's gray-green eyes appear strangely luminous. I can't tell if she's about to cry or if the luster is merely reflected light off the surface of the lake.

"I am not Helga," she says slowly and distinctly. "I am never Helga. You must not call me that again, Isabel. There is no Helga."

"All right," I say slowly, with a worried but patient air, as I link my arm through hers and steer her firmly toward the lake shore. "If you aren't Helga, who are you?"

"I am Lilli," she says pointedly. "My name is Lilli. I am the elder sister of Helga."

# Twenty One

The passport that lies on Minnie Moskin's kitchen table bears a photograph of a shy-looking eleven- or twelve-year-old girl. Her hair, which appears dark in the photo, is cut short and she wears a jacket with a white Peter Pan collar. Her expression is solemn, her eyes turned slightly away from the camera. The face could easily be that of "Helga-who-is-now-Lilli" roughly three years ago.

"So," Ruthie says gently, "you say that this girl isn't you. It's your sister Helga."

"*Ja.*" The girl we must now call Lilli is sitting across from us, clutching a large moist handkerchief and sipping the hot tea that Ruthie's mother has just poured for her. "There was only room for one of us to go on the *Kinder-transport* to England, so it was arranged for Helga, the middle child, to make the escape from Germany. She had Papa's dark eyes and hair. I, Lilli, one year older, and, of course, Elspeth, the youngest, must remain with Mutti, and seek some other means of escape."

Mrs. Moskin brings a platter of her thick cinnamon-and-sugar-sprinkled cookies to the table and urges one on Lilli, who shakes her head politely. "So you went instead of her," she says consolingly, "You still saved one life for your family, for sure. Is that so bad?"

"*Ja*, it is bad. It was not for me, Lilli, to go free and to leave the others surely to die. I made it so that Helga could not go. That is my terrible sin."

"What do you mean, you 'made it so?'" I'm leaning across the table with a doubtful air. Lilli (as it's so hard to think of her now) is always so dramatic, so full of self-blame over things that are really not that terrible. "What'd you do to Helga? I ask with a touch of sarcasm, "break her arm?"

Lilli gives me a startled look. "How could you know that? It was so. Her arm and her shoulder had to be set and put in a cast. We knew the *Kindertransport* would refuse her. The time of departure was too close for it to heal. It was late August 1939. The final transport left on September 1, the day that the war began between Germany and England. So, *Mutti* made me go instead."

"Oh, Lilli," says Ruthie, "I'm sure you never broke your sister's arm on purpose."

Lilli turns away and buries her face in her handkerchief. "We were fighting," she sobs. "All the time we were fighting that summer. Helga would climb under the garden wall to go skating in a small park near the house where we were hidden. It was not safe. Nazi youth often came there, shouting and throwing rocks.

"One day she came home with her forehead bleeding. Another time she ran away, and I ran after her to take her home. I pulled her arm too roughly because of so much danger and how angry I was at her foolishness. She fell down hard and her shoulder, too, was broken."

I stare down once again at the Kindertransport passport, with its three stamped images of the German national symbol, an eagle with its wings outspread, its claws clutching a large ring encircling the Nazi swastika. Helga, the real Helga, looks so mild on the photo. But perhaps, after all, she was the one who was the most ready to fight for the right to live freely, the last to bow to the new rules of Hitler's Germany.

Mrs. Moskin, Ruthie, and I sit in silence. I could tell Lilli over and over again not to blame herself. I could assure her that it was only because she was trying to protect her sister that the accident took place. But I know it wouldn't do any good. It's going to take a long time for Lilli to come to terms with the guilt she feels over what happened to Helga.

"So," I venture, trying to start a conversation, "actually, you're fifteen. You've been fifteen all along. I wonder why that seems so much older than fourteen?"

We are driving through the winter night on dark deserted highways, Lilli and I in the back seat of Mr. F.'s luxurious Cadillac. Late this afternoon, Mr. F. and my father arrived at the Moskin house in Harper's Falls to take us home. But of course Mrs. Moskin and Ruthie wouldn't let us return without serving a meal. So it's now nearly ten P.M.

"*Ja*," Lilli sighs. "Fifteen."

Only two years younger than Roy, I think to myself. But, of course, I don't mention his name. I wonder if she suspects how it was that I tracked her to Harper's Falls. In any case, this is a good subject to avoid, especially now when I'm trying to smooth things out between Lilli and me. But it seems even harder to get "Lilli" to talk to me than when she was "Helga."

I know this is a bad time to ask her questions, but now that Lilli is coming back to live with us, probably until she's old enough to be on her own, I want us to be friends… really friends.

"Did…did I ever do anything horrible to you, Lilli?" I ask hesitantly. "If I ever hurt you or made you talk about things you didn't want to, I'm sorry."

She turns to me warily. "*Nein*, there is nothing."

"See, this is what I mean," I reply, my voice rising in frustration. "I always feel like you're holding something against me and you won't tell me what it is."

Lilli doesn't answer and I exhale a deep sigh.

My father, who is in the passenger seat next to Herman Frankfurter, turns around. "Are you young ladies all right back there? We'll be making a rest stop soon. Just behave yourself, Isabel."

I don't say another word until Lilli and I are in the women's rest room, washing our hands and looking at each other in the mirror over the sink. Maybe it's easier to talk to our images than to each other.

"Lilli, honestly…" I begin.

But I don't get very far. Watching her in the mirror I can see that, for the first time since I've known her, Lilli is looking at me with eyes that are angry and hostile. She starts splashing water on her face in short, violent bursts. "Why did you have to come to that place to look for me, Isabel? Always, always you are following after me. And always, you are asking me questions."

She gulps as she thrusts water from the running faucet into her mouth, "*How did you leave Germany, how did you come to England, what happened to you there?* Always questions, questions," she rants. "Why is my life so important to you?"

"Why?" Doesn't Lilli understand how much our relationship has changed since we first met? Did she even notice how cool I was toward her back in those first days at Moskin's? I was at war with the war then, and I was at war with the whole idea of having "Helga" in my life. So what? I learned some things. People change. That's good, isn't it?

"Listen, Lilli," I reach over and turn off the faucet in her sink, giving it an extra hard twist. "If I ever upset you by being too nosy, I'm sorry. But I had to do it. Because, I was as ignorant as most of the kids at Simpleton Junior High. And plenty of the teachers, too. By asking you all those questions, I learned…so much…"

I stop and take a deep breath, because my heart is pounding and my head is throbbing. "So I'm really thankful for everything you shared with me. And if you want to hate me for the rest of your life, it's okay with me. I think we should go now. My father's probably wondering why we're taking so long."

On a Saturday morning in January, Sibby, Lilli, and I emerge from the subway at Times Square. It's a surprisingly mild day for the middle of winter and a good thing, too, because we head straight for the huge Paramount Theater building, where we're probably going to have to stand in line for hours.

"Never did I see a theater so tall," Lilli remarks looking up from the subway stop to the glass globe atop the baby skyscraper.

Sibby and I smile knowingly. We've been here before and we can hardly wait to see Lilli's face when we walk through the tremendous arch and into the part of the vast building where the block-long movie palace is located. (The upper floors, of course, are offices.)

The inside of the theater is plush with red hangings and glittering gold pillars, high-ceilinged and gorgeously decorated. It seats four thousand people and has an orchestra pit in the basement that can be raised up to the level of the stage for the live show.

"There he is!" Sibby screeches. Beneath the marquee is a huge picture of "Frankie," as she insists on calling him. He's singing with Benny Goodman's band. There's a full-length movie too, starring Frankie's older and more successful rival—so far—Bing Crosby. The "crooner" (that's Crosby) and the "swooner" (that's Sinatra) is what their fans call them.

But ever since Frank Sinatra opened here in the New Year's Eve show on December 31, 1942, he's been the singer everyone's talking about. Girls our own age—bobby-soxers in short skirts, sweaters, and saddle shoes—have been mobbing him. They've been shrieking and moaning and swooning—yes, fainting dead away—over Frankie. This excitement is said to have started in smaller theaters all over New Jersey, including Frankie's home town of Hoboken.

As we join the line of chattering, gossiping, and giggly girls, I can't help wondering what we're doing here in the midst of a world war. Every second that we stand waiting, young men are being killed or wounded or captured on one of the fighting fronts. And those deaths don't even include the unwanted citizens of Hitler-dominated Europe, trapped in the ghettos and in the camps where they are facing the Final Solution.

Yet I suppose that life has to go on. Even though Arnold is now in North Africa, where he's part of a unit that is probably going to invade Italy this summer. Even though Sibby's father is still zig-zagging across the submarine-infested Atlantic with war supplies. Even though Roy (according to Lilli's most recent letter) is now on an aircraft carrier in the Pacific. Even though the war is likely to last for years.

Some things are looking a little better than they did last year, though. I don't think Lilli hates me after all (of course, she still doesn't know I read Roy's letter). For one thing, she's now taking all ninth-grade classes at Simpleton and will soon be going into tenth at the high school. So I'm sticking with my campaign to get her to stand up for herself and stop taking "punishments" for imagined sins. I just hope some day she'll learn that surviving a world disaster, in spite of all its sadness and loss, is nothing to be ashamed of.

When we emerge at last from the darkened theater into the hubbub of Times Square, a wintry dusk is descending. Sibby's flushed cheeks are the same carroty-red as her hair, which is in a terrible state of disarray. We've sat through three shows without daring to go to the bathroom for fear of losing our seats.

"You could have stopped screaming after the first two shows," I remark to Sybil. "You know you're going to be hoarse for days."

"Well," she croaks at me in a stringy voice, "somebody had to show some enthusiasm. You two just sat there and listened to him sing 'That Old Black Magic' like it was the school hymn. Even 'Night and Day' didn't get your juices stirring."

"Never mind us," I reply. "You had plenty of company in that audience. Do you think Frankie might have noticed that Lilli and I were the only ones who weren't howling loud enough to drown him out?"

"I applauded the most loudly I could," Lilli offers apologetically, "because I think he has a very—how you say—dreamy voice. But never before in Germany or one time in England did I hear people become so crazy in a theater. Besides, he is nearly three years already a married man, and he and his wife Nancy have a child. What do these girls who throw their underwear on the stage look for?"

"To me," I add dryly, "his voice is only just okay, a B-minus. Also I can't stand the way his Adam's apple goes galloping up and down when he sings. I have to tell you that that part reminded me of Mr. Jeffers. Also, Sibby, your Frankie's as skinny as a strand of spaghetti and his ears stick out something terrible. And how tall is he anyway, maybe five-feet-seven…and a half."

"I think you're both disgustingly mean to Frankie," Sibby exclaims as we thump our way down the subway steps. "I suppose, Izzie, that you think Billy Crosby is better-looking than Frankie."

"That's a ridiculous comparison. Who knows what Billy will look like when he's as old as Frankie? I hope you realize that your hero is twenty-six. And if the draft boards drop the exemption for married men with children, he might have to go into the Army."

Just then, the train comes thundering into the Times Square subway station and we jump aboard, our three-way argument silenced by the noise.

Later, when I tell Billy about my squabble with Sibby after seeing Sinatra at the Paramount, he just smiles. "Even if Sinatra gets called up," Billy predicts with a knowing grin, "he'll get out of Army duty because of a punctured eardrum, or some such dopey reason. He might get hit with an egg or a rotten tomato now and then. But none a' that will matter. He'll go on to have a great career."

Once again I'm reminded that Billy thinks he knows everything, even if—in this case—he might just be right.

For the time being, though, neither Lilli nor Sibby nor I can agree on the question of Frankie. What, I ask myself, is the reason for all these differences of opinion? And I answer myself in French. *C'est la guerre.*